A Place to Claim as Home

A Place to Claim as Home

by PATRICIA WILLIS

CLARION BOOKS · NEW YORK

Clarion Books
a Houghton Mifflin Company imprint
215 Park Avenue South, New York, NY 10003
© 1991 by Patricia Willis

Willis, Patricia.
    A place to claim as home / by Patricia Willis.
        p.   cm.
    Summary: Thirteen-year-old Henry, hired by the strangely unfriendly Miss Morrison to be summer help on her farm in 1943 while most of the men in the area are overseas in the war, discovers that her gruff hardness conceals hurt over a secret in her past.
    ISBN 0-395-55395-4
    [1. Farm life — Fiction. 2. World War, 1939-1945 — United States — Fiction.]
I. Title
PZ7.W68318P1   1991
[Fic] — dc20

                                                                                90-39693
                                                                                CIP
                                                                                AC
BP   10   9   8   7   6   5   4   3   2   1

This book is for my parents,
Adrienne M. and Clyde L. Bennett,
who gave me the gift
of childhood on a farm.

1
■ ■ ■

The old Packard came to a stop in the dusty road and Henry climbed out. The trip had taken most of the day because Mr. Carver sold farm equipment and had had to stop at several farms along the way. Then they'd spent almost two hours fixing the stalled car. But Henry didn't mind the interruptions. He was in no hurry to get to the Morrison place. Besides, the ride had saved him a fifteen-mile walk.

"Thanks for the lift, Mr. Carver," he said, pulling his suitcase from the backseat.

"Sure, Henry. Sorry about the delay, but this old car breaks down about once a week. Today just happened to be the day."

"If I'd walked, I wouldn't have got here till dark," Henry said. "So thanks again."

He stepped back and waved as the car pulled away, then crossed the road and started up the lane. Past the back corner of the house he spied a thin, ragged figure bent over a hoe. It had to be Miss Morrison. He dropped his suitcase by the front steps and headed around the house. She was hoeing along a row of rambling pea vines, her feed-sack dress sagging like a dirty curtain.

"Hello, Miss Morrison." Dark, glinting eyes turned on Henry. They held no hint of welcome. "I'm Henry Compton." He swallowed hard and forced his gaze to hold steady.

"I'll be in as soon as I finish this row," she said, and turned back to her work.

Henry retreated to the front steps, surprised and a little upset by her blunt dismissal. Maybe she was just tired. Hoeing could take the good humor out of anybody. Tired himself, and hungry, Henry wiped his sweaty face with a bare arm and sat down to wait. He missed Walt and Jack already. They had gone to Grandma's without him and were probably sitting at her kitchen table right this minute dunking homemade sugar cookies in cold milk.

He and Walt and Jack had looked forward to spending the whole summer on Grandma Compton's farm. Since last year they'd been making plans: to build a tree house in the white oak behind the barn; to teach Grandma's young hound, Soapie, to hunt coon; to look for arrowheads in Clark's upper wheat field. But everything had changed in February when their father died.

Henry could still remember those winter days, the quiet in the house, their mother sick, neighbors bringing in food. With Mrs. Compton ill, the three older boys worked and worried and acted as father and mother to the two younger boys and Della. Because Henry was the oldest, he'd taken over the heavy chores. He got the fire going every morning in the cookstove, carried out the ashes, and used the oversized wheelbarrow to bring home jugs of milk and firewood, or coal they picked up along the railroad track. Through the warming days of spring their mother improved, but the family wasn't the same anymore without their father. Henry felt the loss as keenly as the rest of them, maybe because his being an orphan had made no difference to Mr. Compton.

It was during the last week of school that Henry learned about the summer job. The minister had told Mrs. Compton about a woman over near Wynnton who was looking for a boy to stay with her through the summer. Without even consulting Henry, Mrs. Compton had made arrangements for him to take the job.

Henry didn't mind the work. He liked farm work better than any other kind. What worried him was having to live with someone he didn't know, had never even met before. And now that he'd met Miss Morrison, he was more worried than ever. He'd expected her to be friendly, or at least polite, but she seemed almost annoyed by his arrival.

"Come around this way." The woman's clipped words broke into his thoughts, then she vanished around the house. Henry skirted the bushes by the steps, jumping over a plump, dusty chicken that scuttled across his path. Out of the corner of his eye he saw a three-sided woodshed with firewood scattered around it like straws blown up by the wind. A porch swing leaned against one wall.

Miss Morrison was waiting for him on the side porch, and as Henry climbed the stone steps, he sneaked a look at her. Short brown hair fell over a tanned face glistening with perspiration. She was younger than he had thought, but the steady eyes watching him without curiosity seemed old.

She opened the screen door and disappeared into the dark cave of the house. Henry followed, feeling rather than seeing the high ceiling, the linoleum-covered floor, the glowing fire in the stove. In the kitchen's dimness, he saw Miss Morrison pointing to a closed door in the corner.

"You can go up and unpack your things," she said. "The back room will be yours. Turn left at the top of the stairs and go down the hall. The door's open."

As Henry started for the door, she stopped him. "Wait a minute. Slip off those shoes. I don't want dirt tracked upstairs."

Henry did as he was told. He had discovered long ago that every woman had her own set of house rules, and the sooner a fellow learned them, the easier life was.

Steep, shadowy steps wound upward to a bright alcove where the sun, slanting through beveled glass, cast rainbows of light on the faded wallpaper. Henry turned toward the open door at the end of the hall. The room was not large, and the high rounded bed filled half of it. Beside the bed stood an oak stand with an oil lamp on it. The only other furniture was an old platform rocker, its brocade seat worn through to the stuffing. Two tall windows, side by side and framed with white, tied-back curtains, let in enough light for Henry to see the broad oak floor-boards and the closet door.

He crossed to the windows and looked down on several outbuildings aged to ashy gray. A forest of weeds covered the land between them. It would be his job, he guessed, to cut them back.

After hanging his clothes on nails in the closet, he tiptoed back down the hall. Through a window he saw a weathered balcony still bright with sun, and beyond it, the valley, hazy in the descending dusk. Henry had lived his whole life in the hills of eastern Ohio, and though he'd never been to this particular spot before, the green fields and tree-covered hills were familiar and comforting.

Something about the woman, though, made him uneasy. He hoped it was just that he didn't know her yet. Being in a strange house with dark coming on could make any fellow's imagination run wild, he told himself. But he couldn't help shivering as he crept down the staircase toward the kitchen's yellowish glow.

Miss Morrison was stirring something on the stove but turned when she heard him. "You can wash up over there." She pointed to a hand pump over the sink.

Henry lathered his hands, then rinsed them and slicked down his hair. The woman motioned him to the table and placed a steaming dish in front of him. It was dried lima beans cooked down to a thick soup, just the way he liked them.

"I don't cook fancy," she said. "I hope you like beans."

"Yep," Henry said, thinking of the cold egg sandwich he'd eaten while he watched Mr. Carver working on the car. That had been hours ago. The woman poured two glasses of buttermilk, then brought a jar of pickles and a dark crusty loaf of bread to finish out their meal.

As she sat down opposite him, Henry realized he had not yet seen her smile. Even now she was staring into the lamp's flame as though she had forgotten him, and her eyes were dull and faraway. She looked troubled. Maybe she was worried about the farm, Henry thought. He was pretty good at cleaning up, mending broken equipment, putting things in their places, and if he'd known the woman better, he would have told her that. But she'd find it out soon enough.

The beans were delicious. Henry scraped his plate clean, then helped himself to more. The woman ate little and, when she had finished, leaned back in her chair and looked at him.

"I have a big garden and a lot of chickens," she said. "And I just don't seem to have time for all the work. You're not very big," she added.

Henry straightened up in his chair. "I'm pretty strong," he replied.

"We'll see," she said in a flat voice. "I expect you to keep your room straight, and the wood box filled. And the weeds . . . they just got ahead of me. Another thing . . . about the chickens . . . I fasten them up at night because we have foxes around here." When Henry's eyes lighted up, she frowned. "I've been waiting until you came to clean out the chicken house. We'll get at that tomorrow."

Henry nodded. He had already seen plenty of things he could do. He would stack the firewood in the shed and fix the woodshed roof. She probably wanted the porch swing hung, too. And the sooner he got after those weeds, the better.

"The boy who worked for me last summer said he'd be back this year, but he enlisted as soon as he turned eighteen." Miss Morrison sighed. "The boys all want to go to war; they think it's a game. At least you're too young yet to go."

Henry had no desire to go, but he didn't say that to her.

"When the first troops went to Europe, people were saying the war would be over in a year, but it's 1943 already and there's no sign of it ending."

Henry wondered why she was so upset about the war. It was way on the other side of the world and couldn't touch them here.

"Your mother told me you were handy with a hammer," she said. "I hope you're ready to work."

"Yep — uh, yes, ma'am," he murmured.

"No need to call me that. My name is Sarah." Her eyes seemed to bore through Henry. He could hear the tick of the shelf clock like a hammer on an anvil. When she rose and began to clear the table, Henry picked up his plate and glass and carried them over to the sink.

Sarah swung around and her words hit him like a dash

of cold water. "That won't be necessary. I can look after things in my own kitchen."

His face reddening, Henry turned and slipped through the screen door. She was as touchy as an old setting hen. He always helped clear the table at home, and even washed dishes sometimes. She was probably just afraid he'd break something.

Feeling his way down the porch steps, he headed for the woodpile, then stopped to watch a vehicle coming up the valley road, its lights flashing in and out of the trees. He was still watching when it turned into the lane and caught him in its twin beams. Their brightness blinded him, then the lights went out and in the sudden darkness, he heard a door open and shut.

"What're you doing here, boy?" a man's voice growled.

"I'm staying with — with Miss Morrison."

"Since when?" the man demanded.

"I just came today."

"Is she in the house?"

"Yep," Henry said, but the man was already stomping toward the porch.

"Hello, in there," he called. "I come about the chickens."

Sarah appeared at the door, dimly silhouetted in the lamplight. "Evening, Mr. Pickett. That was next week, wasn't it?"

"Just thought I'd stop by and let you know I'll be here early on Tuesday to git 'em."

As the man leaned close to the screen, Henry saw Sarah

draw away from it, folding her arms across her chest. "That's fine," she said. "We'll have them ready."

"How many you gonna have this time?" the man asked, pushing his hands deep in his overall pockets.

"I think there will be at least forty, Mr. Pickett."

Even from where he stood, Henry could hear the man exhale. "I told you before to call me Earl. Hain't nobody calls me Mister."

When the man spoke again his voice was a low whine. "You know, I could come over the night before and help you catch up them chickens. A pretty little woman like you could use a — "

"No! Henry and I can do it. We'll have them ready on Tuesday."

"I seen you got company," the man said, gesturing vaguely toward Henry without looking around. "He gonna stay?"

"Yes. I need help around the place."

"Well, if I'd knowed you wanted someone, I could've sent my son Evan over. He's a whole lot bigger than the boy you got, and he's strong as a mule."

"Thanks just the same, but Henry will do."

Henry smiled in the darkness, thinking her remark could almost be a compliment. Just then he saw the man lay a flat hand against the screen, and he grabbed a few sticks of firewood and hurried up on the porch. Sarah saw him coming and pushed the door open, then shut it behind him.

"We'll look for you on Tuesday, Mr. Pickett," she said.

She did not wait for his reply but turned to the stove and began poking at the fire.

Henry watched from the shadows as the man scowled, first at Sarah's back, then in Henry's direction, and finally turned and melted into the darkness. When Sarah did not speak, Henry went out for another load of wood.

She was standing at the door with a lamp in her hand when he returned. "Mr. Pickett takes my chickens to the sale over at Mt. Strachen," she said. "He's also putting a crop in that field of mine across the road. You heard him mention his son, Evan." She waited for Henry to drop his load into the wood box, then cupped a hand around the lampshade rim and blew out the flame. As she went over and picked up the lamp on the table, she added, "That Evan is a typical boy — obnoxious . . . and a bully, too. I wouldn't have him around."

Henry smiled, thinking that she was joking, but when he saw her eyes the smile faded. She didn't like boys! He couldn't help wondering why she would hire a boy if she thought all of them were obnoxious bullies.

Sarah paused to turn up the lamp's wick, then started for the stairs. "It's bedtime," she said. Henry had no choice but to follow her and the wavering circle of light.

At the door to his room, she stepped aside to let him enter. "If you're not up by eight, I'll call you."

She turned back down the hall before Henry could answer. He undressed and slipped into bed, watching the dancing shadows cast by Sarah's lamp. When a door squeaked shut, he was left in utter darkness, but after a few moments he could make out the double windows framing a black velvet sky. A train wailing in the distance made him think of home. Every night back in Gorleyville the ten o'clock train rumbled through town, blowing at all three crossings. He ground his fists into his tired eyes. Sometimes when he stayed away from home he got home-sick, but that was only at night. When morning came, he felt better.

He thought of his home — not just the big house but the big family, too, the constant noise, and with five boys, the unending horseplay. When Mr. Compton was there, it had been easy for Henry to forget he was an orphan. But from the very beginning Mrs. Compton had been harder to reach, and Henry couldn't help but notice that she treated him differently from her real children. Since Mr. Compton's death she'd grown even more distant, more protective of her own children and less concerned about him. Sometimes he thought that the only mother he'd ever known was really no mother at all. If it hadn't been for leaving Walt and Jack, he might have been almost happy to get away.

Henry's wandering thoughts returned to the dark bed-room and to the odd, brooding woman down the hall. Why was she so sad? He drifted off to sleep remembering that moment when he had gathered up the firewood and stalked past the man, Pickett, in a peculiar attempt to protect her.

$$\frac{2}{\blacksquare\ \blacksquare\ \blacksquare}$$

Henry dressed in the dawn chill and tiptoed down the hall. The house was so quiet that he was sure Sarah must still be sleeping. Downstairs, he crossed to the screen door and let himself out. He could see far down the valley, cornfields coming green, cows grazing along the hillside.

A sparrow landing on the woodshed roof reminded Henry that there was work to do. He began carrying the firewood into the shed and did not quit until every piece was under roof. Then he strolled down the lane to get a better view of the house that would be his summer home. He could see it had been beautiful at one time. Round pillars rose from the front porch to the second-floor balcony, then beyond to weathered gables thrusting upward through the trees. Like a crowning jewel, an attic window mirrored the early morning sun. Despite the peeling paint and blind-darkened windows, Henry thought it looked more like a mansion than an old farmhouse.

Just then, up the valley where the gravel road emerged from the trees, Henry saw a man coming. Tall, and straight-backed despite his years, he walked as if to the beat of some silent music. From his dusty high-topped shoes to his bulging overall pockets, the man was an intriguing sight. Crisp gray hair and a neatly trimmed beard all but hid his features, yet the green eyes were friendly.

"How do, young fellow," the man said as he drew near. "Looks like summer is upon us, wouldn't you say?" Henry nodded and flashed a quick grin.

The man removed a worn leather book from his hip pocket, pulled out a pencil and wrote down something, then returned the articles to his pocket. He pointed to a large, white-breasted bird in a dead tree by the road. "I just wanted to record that red-tailed hawk."

Henry glanced at the tree, then back at the strange man. What was so important about an ugly old red-tail? Hawks were just pesky birds that people shot if they got the chance.

"I gather you don't care much for hawks," the man said with a questioning look.

Henry shrugged. "They kill chickens."

"Not very often," the man said. "It's usually mice or snakes or rabbits."

"I've never seen a hawk up close," Henry said.

"People seldom do. They're afraid of humans. And with good cause," the man added.

"How'd you learn so much about hawks?" Henry asked, strangely at ease with the big man.

"I've studied them and read about them," the man said. "In fact, I've kind of made myself the keeper of the hawks in this valley. People used to think I was crazy, but they're coming around. At least I don't find as many dead or injured hawks as I used to."

"What's in the book?" Henry asked.

"Oh, that's just a kind of census — where and when I see the birds. Say, you're new here. I know everybody in this valley and most of their visiting relatives, too. But I've never seen you before." The man jammed his hands into his pockets and regarded Henry with raised eyebrows.

"I'm working for Miss Morrison. My name's Henry."

"Henry . . . the name of kings and car makers. I have a tabby cat named Henry." The man smiled. "People around here call me Willie. It's mighty nice of you to come and help Miss Morrison."

"I'm getting paid," Henry said.

"Well, that may be, but I would guess you're a fellow who takes his work seriously."

As Henry was wondering how the man could make that judgment when they had only just met, Willie waved a hand toward the house. "I see the woodpile's gone. Now if Miss Morrison had possessed the time or energy to stack all that wood, she'd have done it long ago. So I presume you did it. Is that right?"

"Yep. I just finished. Seemed like a good time to do it."

"Where's your home, Henry?"

"I live over in Gorleyville."

Willie nodded as he studied the farmhouse with narrowed eyes. "So you've come to help her," he said. "Miss

Morrison's had a hard row to hoe. I reckon she's mighty pleased to have you here."

Henry stared. The man certainly didn't know Miss Morrison very well. She was anything but pleased. And why did he think her life was so hard? She had a nice house to live in and plenty to eat. What else did she need?

"I'll do what I can," Henry said.

Willie's green eyes rested on him a moment, then he said, "I predict you'll make some changes in this place, Henry. Maybe the sun is finally going to shine in Miss Morrison's life. Well, I'd better get over to town. Mighty glad to meet you, Henry. I think we'll be friends. So long." Without waiting for a reply, the man marched on down the road, his soft, whistled tune drifting back to Henry.

As he turned back to the house, Henry saw Sarah come out on the porch. She spoke when he came near. "I see you've been at work." She nodded toward the woodshed.

"Yep," Henry said. "It didn't take long."

"Well, we'd better have something to eat, then get started on the chicken house."

After breakfast, they set to work. Henry brought the wheelbarrow from the wagon shed and waited while Sarah unlatched the chicken house door and swung it open. Chickens scurried past them, round-bodied old hens and sleek young pullets. All of them were dirty white with bright red combs and yellow feet.

Henry pushed the wheelbarrow up to the door and stepped inside. The building was divided into two sections by a woven wire partition. A row of wooden nests lined the front wall, and farther back, rough pole roosts rose toward the tin roof. Without waiting for instructions, Henry began to fork the dirty straw into the wheelbarrow. Sarah joined him, working silently, occasionally shooing a hen back outside. Before long, dust thickened the air, swirling in the sunlit doorway and making them both sneeze.

Henry lost count of the loads of manure he wheeled to the field behind the garden, but even when his muscles grew tight and aching, he did not slow his pace. He would prove to the woman that a fellow's size was not important.

At noon they washed in a bucket on the porch, then Sarah brought out a snack of Swiss cheese, thick-sliced bread, new onions from the garden, and ice-cold milk.

"This milk is sure good," Henry said.

"I get it from the Franklins," Sarah said, pointing down the valley to a huge red barn. "They're having a hard time with the work since their son enlisted."

Henry had heard people back in Gorleyville discussing the war with an odd mixture of excitement and bitterness. But he hadn't thought much about it until Martin Connery came home with his sleeve pinned up over what was left of the arm he lost on Guadalcanal. Even so, Martin's injury bothered Henry much less than Sam Connery's enlistment a month later. Sam, quiet, slow-talking, slow to anger, sometimes took Henry and the other Compton boys fishing. He had an uncanny knowledge of fish and they rarely came home empty-handed. Why Sam wanted to go to a war that had caused his brother so much pain was a mystery to Henry.

"Looks like we'll finish by evening," Sarah said. The remark sounded almost optimistic, and Henry looked up, half expecting to see a smile. But her expression was as impassive as ever.

"Yep," he agreed. "You suppose the chickens will appreciate it?"

Sarah's solemn eyes touched his, then bounced away. What would it take to make her smile? Henry could not imagine those tight, pursed lips and cold eyes softening with laughter. Maybe he should add that to his list of summer jobs, making Sarah smile.

With his back to the door, Henry did not see the hen waddle inside until he turned and stumbled over her. Losing his balance, he careened through the doorway, barely missing the wheelbarrow, and sprawled face first among the chickens pecking in the dirt. Chickens fluttered up in all directions, squawking and flapping their wings. One even landed on Henry's head. He cuffed it off and rose up on one elbow, more disgusted than hurt. Then he sat up, spitting and rubbing the dirt from his eyes.

"Dammed chickens," he growled under his breath, then blushed when he saw Sarah in the doorway. A faint spark flared in her eyes like a dying fire coming back to life. As she turned her back, Henry grinned at his own clumsiness, half convinced that Sarah was smiling too.

When all the manure had been hauled away, they brought fresh straw from the barn for the floor and the nests. Then Sarah lured the chickens inside with cracked corn and latched the door.

"I'm glad that's over," she said, swiping at her dusty dress. "One job finished and ten others waiting."

"There's plenty of work on a farm," Henry agreed.

"How would you know?" Sarah demanded. "Don't you live in town?"

"Yes, but my grandma — "

"Boys don't know anything about real work. They just do enough to get by."

Henry stared at her. She certainly wasn't being fair after all the work he'd done, stacking the wood, then helping her with the chicken house. But he'd show her! Whatever else he did this summer, he would prove to her that he was worth his keep and the wages she was paying him.

The next morning after breakfast, Henry went to work on the porch swing. He twisted the ceiling hooks tight, then hung the chains, pulling on them to test their firmness. Sarah must have been watching because she came out to help him raise the swing and hook it to the chains.

When it finally hung level, Sarah sat down and pushed backward, lifting her feet from the floor. "Seems to be all right," was all she said before going back inside.

Henry sat down then, letting his feet dance across the porch floor, each stroke taking him higher and higher. At last he raised his legs and stretched them out from the seat, savoring the movement, the whirr of the chains, the rushing, cooling wind. A porch swing was one of the nicest things about summer, he thought. Too bad Sarah didn't enjoy it.

As the swing slowed and he dropped his feet to the floor, he spied a sickle in the pile of tools on the porch. It was just what he needed to wage war on those weeds. Starting at the edge of the yard, he began to cut, working toward the chicken house and the garden. Thistle and boneset and ironweed fell before him like ripe wheat before a summer storm.

He recalled Grandma Compton's comments on the pesky plants. "Weeds are ambitious," she would say. "They grow night and day, rain and shine, and though they are cut again and again, they refuse to die." Henry smiled, thinking that Sarah's weeds were some of the most ambitious he'd ever seen.

In midmorning, Sarah came down through the yard and pointed to the hill behind the barn. "You see that knoll without trees, just beyond the line fence?" Henry nodded. "There's a raspberry patch up there. It's on Mr. Franklin's property, but he lets me pick them. I'd like you to go up and see how soon they'll be ripe."

"I'll go right now," Henry offered, grateful for a break from the weeds.

At the edge of the barnyard he ducked through the barbed-wire fence. Then he headed up the steep slope, and finally reached the knoll sweating and out of breath. Berries hung plump and plentiful on the bushes. They would be ripe next week for sure and easy to pick, since the paths made last year were still clear. Henry ate the few ripe ones he could find and then, in a half-running, half-walking descent, he returned to the house and reported to Sarah.

After their lunch in the cool kitchen, Henry had to force himself back to the weeds. He had worked only a few minutes when he heard tires sliding in the gravel, then saw a gray pickup truck pull into the field across the road. It must be Pickett, coming to see if there were weeds in his crop. There could be little doubt of that, Henry thought, swinging his sickle in a wide, vicious half circle. Sarah's farm seemed to be one big weed patch.

The hot sun and the monotonous swinging rhythm lulled Henry into a kind of stupor so that he jumped when a voice said, "Hey, whatcha doin'?"

Spinning around, Henry saw a boy in bib overalls standing a few feet away, hands on his hips, teeth clamped on a kitchen match. The boy wore no shirt, and his hefty arms and shoulders were tanned almost black. A skinny girl stood beside him, studying Henry with dark eyes that gleamed through her straggling hair. Her shy smile showed white, even teeth. Henry smiled back at her, then let the smile fade as his glance shifted to the boy he knew would be called Evan.

"I'm cutting weeds," Henry said.

"I seen somebody up on Franklin's hill. Was that you?"

"Yep. Miss Morrison wanted to know how soon the raspberries would be ripe."

"Raspberries is already ripe. I picked some yesterday," the boy declared.

"Well, the berries up there won't be ready till next week," Henry said.

"Evan, them berries you picked wasn't very nice," came the girl's blunt comment. "Most of 'em was green on one side."

With a sudden fury that left Henry gaping, Evan pushed the girl to the ground and stood over her with one arm raised as if to hit her. "You shut up! You don't know nothing about berries," he said.

Henry stepped toward them. "That's no way to treat a little kid," he said.

The big boy turned so quickly that Henry fell back a step. "You keep outa this. It's none of yer business how I treat her."

The boy rolled forward on his toes, eyeing Henry with amusement. "Dad said you was puny. You ain't got enough weight on you to sink a muskrat line. I don't see how you'll ever earn your salt." With that, he turned and waved an arm at the girl. "Git on back to the field." She jumped up and scampered away.

Watching them go, Henry felt a stab of loneliness. It would have been nice to have a friend here, someone he could talk to and go exploring with, but that fellow wouldn't do. In fact, Henry decided, the less I see of him, the happier I'll be.

Thinking of Walt and Jack, Henry longed to be back in Gorleyville, where he knew everyone and everyone knew him.

3
...

Henry went back to the weeds and did not look up until he had cut a swath all the way to the barnyard fence. By that time the blister on his thumb had burst open, and his salty sweat made it burn. That was a good enough reason to quit on the weeds. Besides, there were plenty of other things to do. He should look around and see what kinds of repairs the buildings needed.

After getting a drink in the kitchen, he went to ask Sarah for a hammer and nails. He found her in the garden on her hands and knees, pulling weeds from the dark earth. Her ruddy face and dirty hands somehow softened her, made her look almost pleasant.

"Did I hear you talking with someone?" she asked.

"Yep. Evan was here with his sister."

"Mary Beth?" Sarah's face brightened a little. "She's such a nice child," she said. "But she seems older than nine. Maybe because she's had to look after herself, her mother being sick all the time . . . Oh, here she comes now."

Henry turned. The thin girl strode toward them, an empty bucket rattling against her legs.

"Daddy wants to know, kin we have some water," she

22·

said, as she came up to Sarah. Her gaze flitted to Henry, shy, friendly.

Sarah did not answer but instead stared at a thin line of blood trickling down the girl's leg. "What happened to your knee, Mary Beth? Come here and let me see it."

As Sarah examined the wound, Mary Beth told her, "A stick jabbed me when Evan pushed me down. It ain't nothing."

She looked at Henry and shrugged her shoulders. Remembering how Evan had treated her made Henry angry all over again. But his anger quickly faded because something happened just then that he had begun to think would never happen.

Sarah smiled at Mary Beth. Her eyes took on a warm glow and the corners of her mouth lifted, softening the usual harsh lines. Why, she's pretty, Henry thought. He watched, amazed at the transformation in her, but when she saw him staring, the smile melted away. She stood up and brushed the dirt from her dress.

"Come into the kitchen," she told Mary Beth.

Henry followed them, realizing he had not yet asked about a hammer and nails. He waited on the porch steps until they reappeared, the girl carrying the bucket in one hand and a book in the other. "Much obliged, Miss Morrison," she said.

"You're welcome, Mary Beth," Sarah said. "Be sure to wash that knee when you get home. And there's no hurry with the book."

The girl grinned at Henry as she passed. She went down

the lane with her left arm thrown out from her body to balance the bucket's weight.

"That poor girl. No one seems to care about her," Sarah said.

"You do," Henry said without thinking, then wondered how he could be so bold. "I mean, you're good to her and she likes you."

Sarah's cool gaze riveted on him. "You're very observant, Henry. Do you have any sisters?"

"Yep, one," Henry answered quickly, relieved to take up a safe subject. "Her name is Della. She has a hard time, being the only girl, and the youngest."

"How many of you boys are there?"

"Five. There's Homer, Warren, Jack, and Walt . . . and me. Walt is twelve, a year younger than me. Well, he's really only ten months younger."

"You're only thirteen! Your mother said you were fifteen."

"Well, maybe she did . . . accidentally," Henry said. If his mother had told her that, it was no accident. She was probably afraid that Sarah wouldn't take a younger boy.

Henry got the peculiar feeling that Sarah was reading his thoughts, so he spoke quickly. "Do you have a hammer and some nails?"

Sarah went inside and came out again shortly. She was carrying a claw hammer with a rough, pitted head and one claw missing, and a sack of rusty nails, all sizes mixed together, most of them bent.

24 ·

"I'll get some more nails when I go to the store next week," she said. "You can go with me to help carry my things back."

Henry nodded and had started down the steps when Sarah spoke his name. "Henry, Mary Beth told me about you standing up to Evan. You'd better be careful. He has a bad temper, like his dad."

"I will," Henry said, embarrassed that she knew about the confrontation. Mary Beth probably told her Evan got the best of it, too.

Henry crawled up on the woodshed roof and nailed down the few peeling shingles. Then, dropping some nails into his pocket, he set off to inspect the other outbuildings.

There were lots of loose boards on the wagon shed, and a hole in a corner of the chicken house big enough for a fox to get through. That hole would be his first job. He went to the barn in search of some boards to nail over it. Finding nothing usable on the upper level, he climbed down a vertical ladder to the horse stalls and feed bins below. The cool gloom was refreshing after his stint in the hot sun.

As he stood looking around, dust came sprinkling down from overhead. Falling back a step, he saw a blacksnake slithering along a rafter. Blacksnakes were harmless to people but death on rats and mice, so Henry left it in peace. He found several short boards in one of the wooden feed boxes and was on his way to the chicken house with them when he heard Sarah call him for supper.

While they ate, Henry told her about the blacksnake in the barn.

"Did you kill it?" she asked.

Why was it, Henry wondered, that people always wanted to kill snakes, whether they were poisonous or not? "Nope. If you kill them, the rats will come. Grandma says you can have either blacksnakes or rats."

"That would be a difficult choice," Sarah said, frowning. "Tomorrow we're going to clear that brush pile away from the chicken house. I hope there aren't any snakes in it."

"Blacksnakes won't hurt you," Henry said. "Fact is, they're kinda friendly."

"Friendly!"

Henry jumped at her sudden outburst, and for a moment he thought she was going to laugh at him. He wished she would laugh, even if it was at his expense. But blacksnakes really did help people, no matter what she thought. And if there was one in that brush pile, he'd make sure he found it first and carried it away.

After they had finished eating, Henry got up and, without thinking, took his plate and glass to the sink. Too late he remembered Sarah's stern warning on that first night. He hesitated, then set them in the dishpan. He turned, half expecting to be scolded again, but Sarah had removed the globe from the oil lamp and was busy wiping out the soot.

The next day they worked at pulling apart the jumbled mess of dead tree limbs, rotting boards, and live briars beside the chicken house, and carried the debris out to the open field where it could be set afire without risk to the buildings. Once Sarah yelped and jerked back as a frightened rabbit burst from the brush pile. When the brush had been reduced to a few tangled branches, Henry discovered a litter of baby rabbits, mere days old, bedded down in a fur-lined nest.

"Just leave them there," Sarah told him, and he pulled the grass around the nest so that it was almost invisible again.

"I hope they survive," she said.

"Oh, they will," Henry replied. "The mother rabbit will come back. That's one thing you can count on; a mother always takes care of her young."

He felt for a moment like a man reassuring a child. Then he noticed Sarah's lips tighten into a thin white line, and saw the rake fall from her hands. Her eyes, normally so cold and indifferent, fixed on him, and the flame in them reminded him of hot coals pulsing and flaring in a grate.

Henry stared at her, shocked by the swift change, frightened because he didn't know what was wrong. Sarah stood poised a moment, still as a statue. Then suddenly she spun away in long, lurching strides toward the house.

Henry watched her disappear around the corner of the house. What had upset her so? They'd been talking about the baby rabbits and he'd told her the mother would come back. There was nothing in that to bother a person. He went back to work, watching and waiting for Sarah's return, but there was no sign of her.

When Henry had finished moving all the brush to the open field, he went back to the house for lunch. There was food set out for him on the kitchen table, but no sounds that told of Sarah's presence.

Through the afternoon he worked cutting weeds, his eyes turning often to the silent house. Finally at dusk he saw Sarah come out to lock the chicken house door, but when he went inside a few minutes later, the kitchen was empty. As he ate his solitary supper, he thought of Grandma Compton's bright kitchen. By comparison, this dim, deserted room seemed like a dungeon.

Sarah had breakfast ready when he came downstairs the next morning. Her stone-hard silence warned him not to speak, so he hurried through his meal and went outside. It was plain to see that she didn't want him around. He headed for the sanctuary of the woods with the uneasy feeling that she was watching from a darkened window and was pleased to see him go.

He wandered through the woods, relieved to be alone. After walking for some time, he stepped into a small, sunlit meadow. Someone had been cutting trees there, and not long ago, from the looks of the wilting foliage. Stumps still oozed sap, and their pungent odor, as well as the slender, toothed leaves strewn about, told him the trees had been black walnuts.

He returned to the woods, feeling at ease there, walking and enjoying the solitude. For a time he even forgot Sarah. But his growling stomach reminded him of the passing day. A long, wooded ridge brought him back to the raspberry patch overlooking the farm. Nothing moved down there, not even a breeze in the dark maples. He wondered how Sarah had spent her day. He wished there was something he could do to help her, though why she needed help he didn't know.

Sarah had supper ready when he came back, and they ate in strained silence. Henry had made up his mind that if she asked where he had been, he was going to tell her he'd been looking for berries.

She didn't speak at all, though, until they had finished eating. "We'll be going to town tomorrow," she said at last. Then, looking squarely at Henry with those steely eyes, she asked, "Have you seen the mother rabbit?"

"Nope," he said, "but she's probably back with her babies by now."

"I think you're right. She probably came back as soon as we left."

Henry held his breath and waited, but Sarah did not speak again. It was strange the way those baby bunnies bothered her. Henry cast a quick glance at her, and was relieved to see the usual impassive expression. Though cool and remote, it was still better than the burning hostility of yesterday.

4
∎ ∎ ∎

T he next morning, Sarah counted three dozen eggs into a basket and set it on the table, then disappeared into one of the front rooms. Henry followed as far as the doorway and stood looking in. It was a large room, dark because of the drawn window. blinds, with the musty smell of age and disuse. The couch and two matching chairs, with yellowing doilies on the arms and backs, were lumpy and threadbare. Faded pictures hung on heavy wires from the cornices.

Sarah took a purse from a desk in one corner and turned to leave. Then, when she saw Henry, she stopped in the middle of the room and looked around her, as if trying to see the room as he was seeing it.

"This is a parlor, but I don't use it much," she said. "Grandmother used it when the churchwomen came, and the preacher. That's her," she finished, pointing to a picture over the fireplace. A round-faced woman in a high-collared dress smiled down at Henry.

"She died last spring and I inherited this place. I'm the last of the Morrisons, you know." Her voice was matter-of-fact and did not falter over what struck Henry as a staggering pronouncement. He had never considered that a family could simply die away, become extinct like the dinosaurs.

How must it feel to be the last one, the end of a family line, Henry wondered. When Sarah died, she would take with her the Morrison name and a whole family's history. But maybe she won't be the last, he reasoned; maybe she'll have children, if she ever gets married.

Sarah came downstairs a short while later wearing a yellow and white dress and carrying a yellow straw hat. She reminded Henry of the stylish women in the Sears, Roebuck catalogue. If it weren't for the dullness in her eyes, he thought, she would be almost pretty.

Sarah picked up the basket of eggs and they set off for town, walking beneath arching trees that dappled the roadway with light and shadow. They were nearing Franklin's farm before Sarah spoke, seeming to take up a previous conversation where she'd left off.

"You know, it really doesn't matter how old you are. I wanted a boy who could work, and I see you can do that."

Henry flashed her a quick smile. "I'm just glad I got the chance to earn some money."

"Your mother said I was to pay her the wages."

"She needs the money for the family," Henry said.

"Yes, it's hard for a widow to raise a family alone," Sarah said. After a few moments of silence, she continued.

"You being her first son, she must depend on you a lot."

"I guess so . . . but . . . I'm not really her first son," Henry corrected her, then instantly wished he had let the misconception pass.

"I thought you said you were the oldest."

"I am, but . . . What I mean is, she's not my real mother."

"Oh!" For the first time since he'd met her, Sarah looked surprised.

"Well, Mr. Compton got me from the Children's Home. He'd gone there to fix the roof and he found out there was hardly enough food to go around. I was only four, and being the smallest, I got the least to eat. He said I was skinny as a hoe handle." All Henry could see of Sarah's face was her impassive profile.

"Then you don't remember your real parents?" she asked.

"Nope," he said. The Comptons had taken him in and given him a home, and he'd felt no need even to wonder about two strangers he would never meet.

They walked on in silence until Sarah left the road and started down a well-worn path. "I usually take the short-cut over the trestle," was all she said. The path led past Mr. Franklin's barn, then up a cinder bank to the railroad bed. Stepping between the shiny rails, Henry paused to look up the track, then down, before falling in behind Sarah.

The wooden trestle bridged a muddy, tree-lined creek. Through the lattice of thick oily timbers, Henry could see swirling water far below. He tried to still his fluttering stomach. It couldn't be more than twenty steps to the other side, but it looked like a mile. He turned his head to listen for the sound of a train, vowing that if he heard one coming he would run for solid ground, no matter what Sarah might do.

Just beyond the trestle they came to the town, not a real town laid out in neat measured blocks, but a random gathering of houses clinging to the railroad like melons to a vine. They left the tracks and crossed a dusty road, then climbed steep wooden steps to the general store. Out front was the usual merchandise, tools, a stack of tires, shiny new cans and buckets, watched over by two old men on a wooden bench. As Sarah passed inside, one of the men winked at Henry and said, "You're Miss Morrison's new hired hand, I reckon."

"Yep," Henry said, throwing back his shoulders a little. He grinned and slipped through the screen door into a large, noisy room where people milled about, talking and laughing. He could see Sarah in the back of the store, counting out her eggs. Knowing she wouldn't need him for a while, he strolled around the store with the freedom of a boy ignored by busy adults.

"Hello, Henry." He jerked around to see Willie's friendly smile. "What are you buying today?" the man asked.

"Miss Morrison's doing the buying. I just came along to help carry."

Just then a thin, neat man in a brown striped suit

walked over to them, rested both hands on his gold-handled cane, and spoke to Willie. "Howdy, Major. Seems to me I remember you spent some time in the Pacific."

"Yes, I did, Mr. Jones," Willie said, "but it was several years ago."

"My grandson's out there somewhere. He's a marine. Been in the thick of things about two months," the man said proudly. "In his last letter he said he'd just finished taking a bath in a river, the first time in nine days he'd changed clothes. He wrote more, but they censored it. I think he was trying to tell us about the fighting."

"Yes, they'd have to cut that out," Willie said. "From what I hear, the malaria is giving the men almost as much trouble as the Japanese."

"Well, if Teddy has half a chance, he'll kill his share of those Tojos. Killing is what war is all about, isn't it, Major?"

"Yes," Willie agreed. "It's a poor means of settling differences, but we haven't learned a better way yet."

As the man moved on, Henry blurted out, "You were a soldier?"

"I served in the army until they put me out to pasture," Willie said. "Now when they need me, I'm too old." Henry could only stare in admiration. He'd never met a real army officer before.

"I'm going to treat you to an ice cream cone before you leave," Willie said, "but first I want to talk to Sarah." He went off to find her while Henry resumed his tour of the store. He stopped at the ice cream counter. The sign said they had vanilla, chocolate, strawberry, and butter pecan, but there was no need for deliberation. He always chose chocolate.

"You gonna git some ice cream?" a grating voice inquired. Henry turned to face Evan. The boy looked the same as he had at Sarah's farm, eyes unblinking, hands on his hips, a match between his teeth. Henry wondered if he was going to cause more trouble.

"Afterwhile I am," Henry said.

He could not help but stare at the ugly bruise on Evan's cheek. Evan lifted a hand and touched it gingerly. "A horse kicked me," he explained, though Henry had not intended to ask.

"It must hurt bad," Henry said.

"It ain't nothin'." Evan's words struck a familiar chord in Henry. Those were the exact words Mary Beth had used to describe her bleeding leg. "Dad says we're gonna give you and old lady Morrison a ride home."

Henry would've preferred to walk, but then he remembered the railroad trestle and decided the truck would be better after all. He turned to study the ice cream list again, wishing the fellow would disappear. Strangely, when he looked around moments later, Evan was nowhere in sight.

After Henry and Willie got their cones, they sat on tall stools and leaned on the dark wooden counter.

"You remember that cat I mentioned the other day,"

Willie said, "the one named Henry? Well, I found out he's sired a peck basketful of kittens. I wonder if you might want one. Sarah said it would be all right."

Henry was too surprised to speak, but he managed to nod his head, grinning all the while.

"Good," Willie said. "I'll bring one down on my next trip."

Never in his whole life had Henry owned a real pet. Once he caught a half-grown coon, but turned it loose again, ashamed to keep the wild thing in a cage. This was different! Cats were pets from the moment they were born. He wondered why Sarah didn't already have a cat. Every farm ought to have at least one. Besides, it would have been some company for her. Well, when Willie brought his kitten, it would be company for both of them.

A minute or two after Willie left, Henry saw Sarah coming toward him with a look on her face that was almost pleasant. Right then he made up his mind that as soon as they got home he would tell her how pretty she looked.

"Mr. Pickett's going right past the farm, so when you finish your cone, you can help me carry the things out to the truck."

Once Sarah's packages were stowed, she climbed into the cab. Henry and Evan slid into the back and rode with their feet dangling over the tailgate. The old truck rumbled through a covered bridge. Then it took the washboard road along the hillside, past dusty houses hunched on the lower side of the road, their front porches only inches from the roadway, their back porches sagging down the crumbling bank toward the creek.

"There's catfish in that crick. I caught a four-pounder last fall," Evan said, raising his voice above the truck's roar. Henry nodded but said nothing.

"You don't talk much," Evan said. Henry shrugged his shoulders and looked away.

"You oughta git along fine with old lady Morrison. She don't talk much either. Anyway, folks just leave her alone. She made her bed, now she has to sleep in it."

"What do you mean?" Henry demanded.

"You sure ain't up on things, are you? Didn't anybody tell you about her 'fore you come here?"

Evan's tone goaded Henry into the question, "Tell me what?" He hated the way Evan grinned and ran his tongue along the inside of his lower lip.

"Well, some years back she was sent here to stay with her grandma 'cause she done something real bad." Evan let go of the last word with maddening slowness. When Henry did not speak, he went on. "Everyone knew she was gonna have a baby. She wasn't married neither. The baby died when it was only a few days old. Some say it was God's punishment; some say she smothered it 'cause she didn't want it."

Satisfied with his story, Evan leaned back on his hands, grinning.

Henry could not help but turn and stare at the woman

in the truck cab. Was it possible she could do such a thing? He remembered the baby rabbits they'd found and Sarah's strange concern for them. How could she care so much about baby bunnies and not care anything about a real baby?

"Don't you think she acts mighty strange?" Evan asked.

"She seems all right to me," Henry said, at the same time admitting to himself that Sarah did act as if she guarded some dark secret.

Evan took off his straw hat, swiped at the inside sweatband, then set it back on his head. "Like it or not, you're living with a whore and a murderer," he said to Henry.

Just then the truck rolled to a stop at the Morrison place.

5
...

Henry did not look at Evan again, but grabbed the packages and started up the lane. Sarah was speaking to Pickett as she slid to the ground. "We'll have them ready at daylight." Henry had forgotten all about the chickens. He'd have to help her catch the ones for the sale after dark, but just now he had to get away by himself. He went inside and dumped the packages on the kitchen table, then hurried out the door before Sarah got to the porch.

He almost ran toward the barn. Just when he was getting to know Sarah, even like her a little, Evan came along and spoiled everything. He hated Evan for telling the story about her and for calling her those names. But could it all be true? Was she a murderer?

Maybe Evan sensed that Sarah didn't like him and had made up the tale to get even with her. Somehow, Henry had to find out the truth. He thought of Willie. If anyone would know the truth of it, Willie would. Meanwhile, he had to go back to the house and face Sarah as if nothing had happened. Less than an hour ago he had been thinking how pretty she was, but now her face hovered like a black cloud in his mind.

He could not bring himself to look at Sarah during supper; his eyes simply refused to rise any higher than the tabletop. As soon as the meal was over, he slipped outside and sat down on the porch step. The fog rising out of the bottoms, a thin white mist ebbing and flowing with every breath of air, filled him with a nameless fear.

When it was full dark, Sarah brought an oil lamp to light their way to the chicken house. The old setters huddled in their nests, while the younger chickens hunched on the pole roosts, clucking softly, blinking in the lamplight.

Gently they carried the ones for the sale behind the wire partition and set them on the roost. Still upset by Evan's tale, Henry worked in silence, and when Sarah spoke to him, he answered without looking at her. He felt a dull ache in his stomach that just wouldn't go away. He couldn't tell if it was from disappointment or fear.

When forty-three chickens were transferred to the holding cage, they secured the door and started for the house. Sarah led the way, her feed-sack dress flapping against her legs. Once she turned to see if Henry was coming, and above the lamp's flame her face was a grotesque skull with black holes for eyes. At that moment Henry would have believed she was capable of anything.

After his bath, Henry started to bed, but Sarah stopped him. "Did you and Evan get along all right today?"

Henry didn't want to think about Evan. "I don't know if anyone can get along with him," he muttered. "Not even animals. He had a bruise on his face where a horse kicked him."

He heard Sarah's breath come out in a sigh. "More than likely his father hit him," she said. "That man has a terrible temper. I'm surprised he hasn't murdered someone before this."

Henry stared at her. How could she talk so easily about murder? Had she forgotten what she'd done? Then he turned away, upset because for a moment he had believed Evan's story.

After he crawled into bed, Henry mulled over the events of the day that had started so routinely and then had turned into catastrophe. But nothing had really changed. If there was a catastrophe, it had happened years ago. He pulled the quilt up to his chin and closed his eyes, hoping he could fall asleep.

Thunder woke him the next morning, not the deafening claps of a summer storm but a heavy rumbling growl, like an iron-wheeled wagon rolling down a brick road. On his way downstairs he paused at the balcony door to watch the first soft raindrops strike the balustrade. It was an all-day rain for sure, so the repairs to the chicken house would have to wait.

The sound of a vehicle coming up the road made him hurry down the steps. Sarah was already at the door. "It's Mr. Pickett," she said, and draped a piece of an old blanket around her shoulders before stepping out on the porch.

"Good morning," she said to Pickett.

"It hain't too good a morning," he replied, leaning an elbow on the frame of the open truck window. "'Course rain's better than no weather at all." He grinned, but when Sarah's expression did not change, he pulled a match from his shirt pocket and clamped it between his teeth. "Can I back my truck out there?" he asked, waving a hand toward the chicken house.

"Yes, there's nothing there but weeds," Sarah replied, starting down the steps. Henry followed, hunching his shoulders against the misting rain.

Pickett backed the truck up close to the doorway, then came around and wrestled three flat crates onto the tailgate. He turned to Sarah. "Well, let's git 'em loaded. I got a lot to do today."

It took only a few minutes to catch the chickens and load them into the crates. As Henry scrambled after the last one and trapped it against the wire partition, his arm scraped across a sharp-edged wire. He saw blood bubble up and run down his arm.

Sarah took the chicken from him, silently eyeing the wound. "That's all of them," she said to Pickett. He pushed the crates forward and latched the tailgate. Then, with an irritable glance in their direction, he got in the truck and drove off.

Sarah led the way through the drizzle to the porch. She slipped off her muddy shoes while Henry rinsed his feet under the rainwater pouring from the roof. He held his arm under the waterfall and the blood disappeared.

"I think we'll go to the attic today," Sarah said. "I've been wanting to pack some things away ever since Grandmother died. But first you need a bandage on that arm, then we'll have some breakfast." She spoke of her grandmother's death in a dull, unfeeling voice, as if she were talking about a stranger. Had she disliked her grandmother, Henry wondered.

Inside, Sarah motioned him to a chair. With her usual cool efficiency, she cleansed the wound with warm water, dabbed some salve on it, and wrapped it in a white cloth. The gentleness of her touch was unexpected, and while she worked, Henry secretly studied the face so near to his own. Tiny wrinkles fanned out from the corners of her eyes, and a frown of concentration creased her forehead. He could see a few freckles almost hidden beneath her deep tan. Up close, she looked young and, he thought, a little sad. He felt again that odd protectiveness he had felt the day he arrived at the farm. How would he feel if she really was a murderer?

After breakfast, Sarah led the way through an upstairs hall door and on to the top floor. The attic was one large room illuminated by windows midway in each wall, with rough beams rising to the roof's peak.

Henry held his breath and listened to the gentle patter of rain on the slate roof. "It sure is a big house," he said.

"And well built, too," Sarah replied. "The lumber was cut here on the farm. Oh, did Willie tell you about the lumber truck?" When Henry shook his head, she went on. "The other evening about dusk he saw a truck loaded with logs pull out of the old abandoned road that separates his property from mine. He thinks someone may be cutting trees on our land."

"You mean . . . stealing them?"

"It looks that way. Grandmother never sold off any of the timber and neither have I. But I'd planned on cutting enough this year to make the mortgage payment."

"I saw where some trees were cut," Henry said.

"Where?"

"Over that hill behind the barn."

"Oh, no! I'll bet they took the walnuts I had marked for cutting." She sank down on an old straight chair as if a heavy hand had pushed her there.

"You've got plenty more trees on the farm," Henry said, hoping to cheer her up.

"But walnuts bring the best price," she said, "and I need almost eleven hundred dollars."

"Maybe they'll catch the thieves and you'll get your logs back."

Sarah stood up and rubbed a hand across her forehead. "Maybe," she said, "but it's not too likely. Anyway, worrying never changes anything. We'd best get to work."

All attics looked alike to Henry. Boxes, chests, odd chairs, tables, old shoes, lampshades, picture frames, and jars of all sizes and colors were just what he had expected to see.

They worked side by side, speaking only when necessary, filling boxes and stacking them under the eaves. Beneath an old chair Henry discovered a wooden picture frame not much bigger than his hand. Dust had filtered under the glass and partially obscured the photograph, but he could still make out a man seated in a straight chair and a pretty girl standing beside him, her hand resting on his shoulder. She wore a high-collared dress and she was smiling.

When he handed the picture to Sarah, she said, "That's Grandmother on her wedding day." Her voice and the way she tenderly rubbed the glass told Henry that she had loved her grandmother after all.

"They were married less than a year when he died," she said. "Grandmother never got over losing him. She lived the rest of her life with just a memory." After a pause, she added, "Of course, she did have the baby . . . my father."

Henry cast a quick glance at her, but her eyes were hidden under lowered lashes. He would have given a dollar to know what she was thinking. That gave him an idea. Maybe he could find out something from Sarah herself, some fact that would refute Evan's story.

"When did you come here?" he asked, trying to make his question sound casual.

"It was 1929, just after the stock market crash. My father died in 1930 and my mother a few months after him. I've been here ever since."

"You were lucky to have your grandmother."

"I didn't like it here at first, but I got used to it after a while. Anyway," she went on, "we go where we have to go." Henry agreed with her. He'd never had much to say about where he lived, either.

"Now there aren't any Morrisons left except me, and when I die, this farm will probably go to some distant relative who never even knew a Morrison."

"You may not be the last Morrison," Henry said. He didn't realize his words would sound so blunt. He flinched at the ice in Sarah's eyes.

"What do you mean?" she asked.

"Well, you . . . uh . . . you might get married," Henry said, "and have some children."

"Oh, that's not likely," she said, her gaze dropping to the old photograph. "Marriage is out of the question for me."

"But you can't tell — " Henry began.

"I won't marry. I don't want any children." Her gruff tone squelched any further argument. The fact that she didn't like children was no surprise. Henry watched out of the corner of his eye as she walked over and stood gazing out the window.

When she spoke again, her voice was barely audible over the driving rain. "People shouldn't have children if they don't want them." Henry stared at her dark silhouette, holding his breath. "My mother never wanted me," Sarah continued. "She said I was an accident because she never planned to have any children."

46 ·

"Well, my mother . . ." Henry hesitated, then went on, "uh . . . the mother I have now . . . I don't think she wanted me to live with them. She treats me all right, but I can tell." Strange, that he should tell her that when he'd never admitted it to anyone else.

"We're birds of a feather, I guess," Sarah said.

"Yep," Henry agreed, then grinned and added, "I reckon you could call us cowbirds."

"Cowbirds?" She frowned at him.

"Well, cowbirds lay their eggs in other birds' nests and then just leave 'em for the other birds to raise."

A shadow seemed to move across Sarah's face. Henry hurried on, afraid that she had misunderstood him. "Cowbirds get by all right," he said, "even though their real mothers don't raise 'em."

Sarah turned her face away, then pushed a box roughly aside on her way to the stairs. "I'm going down to fix some lunch," she said.

"Damn it!" Henry muttered when she had gone. He had said something wrong again. He stood there looking out at the rain, wishing he could explain that he had not meant to hurt her.

Sometime later she called him to eat. Two helpings of the thick homemade noodles simmered in chicken broth lifted his spirits a little. "Those raspberries ought to be about ripe," he said, "but I guess they'll need a day to dry off."

"If it ever stops raining," Sarah sighed. "I suppose we

should be thankful for the rain. It'll make the garden grow."

"And the weeds," Henry added with a grin.

"You have a knack for seeing the sunny side of life, Henry."

Her simple statement, along with her look that was almost a smile, stayed with Henry the rest of the day.

6
...

The rain had stopped during the night, and dawn revealed fresh fields beneath a bright blue sky. Henry tiptoed down the hall and stopped by the balcony door. With a trembling hand, he turned the glass knob, and when the door clicked open, he slipped out onto the balcony. Tatters of mist floated below him, but his gaze swept outward and away. Something about a balcony compelled a person to lift his head and throw back his shoulders. Henry understood why ancient kings built watchtowers in their castle walls.

"Grandmother loved this balcony," came Sarah's voice from the doorway. Henry spun around, red-faced at being caught, but she apparently saw nothing wrong with his being there.

She came to stand beside him, then after several moments pointed down the valley. "If you look just to the right of Franklin's barn, between the barn and that big tree, you can see the top of the church spire. I suppose you went to church back home," she said.

"Yep. We filled a whole pew," Henry said, remembering how people used to call them the Compton choir.

"I go over some Sundays, depending on the weather," she said.

Sarah was different from his mother, who accepted no excuse for absence from church. The Comptons went, rain or shine.

After breakfast, Henry brought in a load of firewood, then took the old hammer and the sack of bent nails and headed for the chicken house. He opened the door and the chickens rushed outside, all except the jealous hens guarding their eggs.

He went to the back of the chicken house and was just getting ready to nail a board over the hole when Sarah came around the corner. "I got some new nails," she said, handing him the heavy sack.

Henry pounded a new nail into a board, then laid it against the wall. Before he could get it nailed in place, it slipped from his grasp.

"Here, let me hold that," Sarah offered. Henry hammered gingerly at first, as if he were pounding old nails and expected them to bend. But the new nails drove straight and solid and he was soon swinging with confidence.

"Your mother was right," Sarah said. "You know how to use a hammer."

"This ought to keep out any fox looking for a chicken dinner," he said, trying to hide his pleasure.

"I hope so. The eggs are about ready to hatch. We'll have to keep a close eye on the peeps."

"Yep. There's a hawk hunts around here pretty regular. Willie likes hawks," he added.

"Well, they've never bothered my chickens, but I still don't trust them."

While Henry finished nailing on the second board, Sarah stepped back and looked up at the chicken house roof. "I noticed the other day it was raining in by the nests," she said. "Do you think you can get up there to fix it?"

Henry nodded and looked around for something to stand on to reach the overhang. He leaned one of the scrap boards against the wall and started walking up it, hands gripping the sides, toes curling for traction.

"Wait a minute," Sarah said. "I'll steady it for you."

Henry inched up the wobbly board, felt it sag under his weight; then suddenly it snapped in two and he went tumbling down, taking Sarah with him. They landed in a confused tangle in the weeds, Sarah on her side with one arm pinned under her. Henry rolled up to his knees and looked into bright, sparkling eyes.

"You're either falling out of this chicken house, or off of it," she said, laughter breaking up her speech.

Henry could only stare. That day he'd fallen out the door he'd seen just a hint of a smile; now she was actually laughing out loud. Henry grinned back at her.

"Do you call this working?" The man's scolding voice

took them by surprise. Willie was standing a few feet away with his hands in his pockets, and he began to laugh too.

Sarah got to her feet, brushing at her dress. "Henry was trying to get up on the roof."

"It looked to me like he was trying to get down," Willie said, still laughing. "Here, I'll give you a hand." He turned his palms up and interlaced his fingers, making a secure step for Henry's bare foot. Henry stepped into it and felt himself boosted easily to the roof.

As Willie passed up the hammer and nails, Sarah said, "I forgot; I've got bread rising. You stay and have lunch with us, Willie."

After nailing down the loose pieces of tin, Henry dropped the hammer and nails to Willie. Easing his legs over the roof edge, he felt his foot captured in Willie's big hands. Once on the ground, he grinned at Willie and said, "I'm glad you came along."

"I am too," Willie said. "It's the strangest thing. I can't remember when I've seen Sarah laugh like that."

Now was the time to ask him about Sarah, Henry thought, but before he could figure out how to begin, Willie spoke again. "Henry, I've got an extra passenger here I'd like to get rid of." He reached in behind the bib of his overalls and drew out a small tabby kitten. It had black stripes running the length of its body and a fluffy, nervous tail. When Willie placed the soft creature in Henry's outstretched hands, it nosed his fingers, then sat down and began to purr.

"It's up to you to name him," Willie said. "I ran out of names before I ran out of cats."

Sarah met them at the screen door and, spying the kitten, came out on the porch. "Is this our new mouser?"

She reached out and rubbed the kitten's ears. Watching her, Henry thought she looked different somehow, more alive, as if the earlier laughter had tapped some hidden spring of vitality.

While they ate lunch, the kitten remained just outside the screen door, mewing, testing the screen with its nose. Henry's gaze returned to it again and again. As a result he heard only fragments of Sarah and Willie's conversation until he realized they were talking about the timber thieves.

"I followed their tracks along Blackwood Creek. They cut three big oaks on my back hill and hauled them out through Lamper's Quarry," Willie was saying.

Sarah glanced at Henry. "Henry found a cut too," she said, then paused to let Henry tell it.

"Well, the other day when I was out in the woods, I came across a clearing with about seven new stumps. Walnuts."

"Where was it, Henry?" Willie asked.

Henry pointed to the woods behind the barn and said, "I don't know exactly, but I could show you."

"That's a good idea," Willie replied. "We'll walk back there this afternoon. Then I'll notify the sheriff."

Henry led the way past the chicken house and into the shady woods. At the barbed-wire fence he pushed down the bottom strand with his foot, lifted the middle strand,

and waited for Willie to duck through. Willie did the same for him, then they continued on in comfortable silence. When they passed through another fence, Henry indicated that they were getting close to the clearing.

"Well, we're still on Sarah's land," Willie said.

The mention of her name reminded Henry of his plan to find out about Sarah. He asked his question without looking at Willie. "How long have you known Sarah?"

"I met her in 1929 when she came to live with her grandmother. I had moved here in 1927 after retiring from the service. I'd just lost my wife and didn't know anyone around here. But when I met Mrs. Morrison, we were friends right from the start. She was a fine person, and good to Sarah, too." After a moment he asked, "How are you and Sarah getting along?"

"Well, we . . . uh . . . we're doing all right . . . but . . ."

"What's the problem, Henry?"

Henry stopped and faced Willie, but even under the man's gentle gaze, the words did not come easily. "The other day Evan told me . . . He said that Sarah — I mean, he said she'd been sent here because she had — she was going to have a baby."

Henry's face felt as hot as a stove lid and he looked away into the trees.

It seemed as if hours passed before Willie spoke. "I suppose you were bound to hear things," he said. Then, with a soft grunt, he sat down beside a beech tree and leaned back against the smooth gray trunk. He pulled a red bandana from his hip pocket and wiped his face. "Yes, Sarah was expecting a child when she came here," he said at last.

Henry breathed a sigh. Then it was true! But he was determined to learn the whole truth.

He dropped down beside Willie. "Evan said that she — that people said she . . . killed her baby." His fearful gaze fastened on Willie. "What happened to the baby?"

There was a long silence as Willie picked up a dead leaf and smoothed it between his fingers. Finally he turned a piercing gaze on Henry. "Sarah has suffered a lot in her young life," he said. "What I tell you has to be kept confidential . . . for her sake."

Henry nodded, feeling his stomach tighten as he waited for the secret to unfold.

"When Sarah's parents learned Sarah was going to have a baby, they sent her to live with her grandmother to avoid all the embarrassment," Willie said, "and they insisted that she get rid of the baby." When Henry's eyes widened in horror, Willie said, "Oh, no, not the way Evan tells it. Doc made arrangements for . . . for . . . uh, a young couple to take Sarah's baby."

Henry expelled his breath, not realizing that he had been holding it. "I knew it! I knew she couldn't do that." He beamed at Willie. Sarah was not a murderer; she had not killed her baby.

Suddenly he realized that there were still a lot of questions, though. "Didn't Sarah want the baby?" he asked.

Sarah's own words went spinning through his mind: *I won't marry. I don't want any children.*

"You have to understand, Henry, that she was a confused young girl, deeply hurt because her parents had sent her away. It wasn't easy for a single girl to face all that alone," Willie said. "Maybe she made the best decision after all."

Henry plucked a blade of grass and clamped it between his teeth, trying to picture Sarah as a girl. He remembered her saying that both of her parents had died that year. Henry wondered if they had come to visit her those last months and if they had finally forgiven her.

Willie stood up and brushed the seat of his pants. "Remember, Henry, you're not to discuss this with anyone. I don't want to see Sarah hurt any more."

"I don't either," Henry replied, wondering what he could do about Evan. Henry guessed Evan told his outrageous tale to anyone who would listen.

Moving through the woods in silence, he and Willie soon came to the man-made clearing. It was as Henry had seen it last time, a sun-dappled meadow dotted with stumps, but now the discarded foliage lay crisp and brown.

"They stole some nice ones," Willie said, running a hand over a rough-cut stump. He and Henry followed the tracks up the slope to the top of the rise. Willie sighed and said, "There's no need to go farther. They just pulled onto the township road down by the old Dunlap mine. They know this land very well."

"Is this still Sarah's land?"

"Yes, her property runs to the road back there," Willie said.

They retraced their path through the woods, talking little, each lost in his own thoughts. But as they neared the farm, wild inhuman squeals broke into the quietness, and they hurried ahead to see what was wrong.

Sarah was chasing a huge black hog around the yard, beating on its back with a stick. The sow grunted and wheezed and tried to stay out of reach while several smaller pigs roamed the yard, indifferent to their mother's distress. The reason for Sarah's anger was obvious. The family of pigs had come into the yard and had rooted up large areas of sod until the yard looked like a newly spaded garden.

Sarah saw Willie and Henry and threw up her hands. "I was working inside when I heard the grunting. They had done most of their damage by the time I got out here."

"They're Franklin's, aren't they?" Willie asked.

"Yes," Sarah said. Then she clapped her hands at the pigs, shouting in a voice Henry had never heard before, "Go home! Get out of my yard!"

Willie took Sarah's stick and turned the big sow toward the road with light taps on her neck and back, while Henry herded the young pigs along behind. Once in the road, they seemed to know they were going home and needed little urging. When the strange caravan reached Franklin's farm, the pigs waddled through a partially opened gate into their pen. Mr. Franklin, a thin man with a receding hairline and mild blue eyes, came out of the barn shaking his head.

"I appreciate you bringing her back, Willie. She's a real roamer. I'd get rid of her if she wasn't so good at raising her litters." He pulled the gate shut and looped a wire over the gatepost. "Did they do any damage?"

"Rooted up some of the sod in the yard," Willie replied.

"Looking for grubs, I reckon," Mr. Franklin said. "Will you tell Miss Morrison I'm awfully sorry and I'll be glad to come and help her replace it."

"Oh, it's not that bad," said Willie. "Henry can fix it in half an hour."

"Is this Miss Morrison's helper?" Mr. Franklin asked, looking over at Henry and smiling.

"That's right. Henry Compton from Gorleyville," Willie said.

"Welcome, Henry. Hope you like our valley."

"Yep, I sure do," Henry said. Then for a minute they all turned and watched the grunting, rooting pigs in their muddy pen.

"What do you hear from Lyle?" Willie asked.

"Last letter he was somewhere in North Africa. I think he must be in the desert. He said during the day it got so hot, they could fry an egg on the jeep hood. Said he was sorry to miss the spring planting."

"I bet," Willie said. "You and Lyle always managed to get your corn in before anyone else in the valley."

"That was mostly Lyle's doing," Franklin said. "I was lucky just to get my bottomland in this year."

"Lyle will probably be here for next year's planting," Willie said. "This war can't last forever."

"No, but it's lasting long enough to kill off some of our best men," Franklin said. Willie nodded his agreement as he and Henry turned to go.

That evening at supper, Henry studied Sarah with new eyes. She was as he had always known her, quiet, pensive, lost in the world of her own mind. He tried to picture her as the bewildered young girl who had been banished to this place in disgrace. How lonely she must have been, with only an old woman for company.

And what about the baby? Henry had a reasonable understanding of babies and where they came from, after taking care of the animals on Grandma's farm. Still, he knew it was different with people. Two people married and had children because they loved each other. Who was the man Sarah had loved, and why didn't they get married. Where was he now? The avalanche of questions made Henry's head spin.

He thought of young Wilma Cross who had quit school when she got pregnant. Unlike Sarah, Wilma had kept her baby boy and lived on with her folks. The baby was welcomed into that family as warmly as if he'd been planned. And despite the scorn of some of Gorleyville's solid citizens, Wilma and her baby had both grown up happy.

Anyone could see why Sarah was not happy, living by herself this past year, suffering people's silent contempt, having no friends except Willie. People left her alone, as Evan put it, because she had made a mistake. Well, Henry thought, if they were going to treat Sarah as an outcast whether she kept her baby or gave it away, she might as well have kept it.

7

∎ ∎ ∎

I t was a perfect day for picking berries, sunny, with a
light breeze, and Henry was eager to get started. Sarah
gave him a bucket and she carried a small wooden-handled
kettle. They crossed the barnyard and began their climb.

Halfway up, Sarah stopped to catch her breath and
gaze down at the tree-shrouded house. "The place looks
run down, doesn't it?"

"It'll look better when the weeds are gone," Henry said.

"A farm runs best with a family on it," she declared.
"There's something for everyone to do, no matter what
age they are."

It occurred to Henry that if she had kept her baby, she
would have some family to help her now. He wondered
why he hadn't thought to ask Willie when her child was
born, and whether it was a girl or a boy.

Henry reached the raspberry patch first and, finding
few berries, circled around the edge looking for more.
Sarah worked her way into the middle until the tall
tangled briars hid her from view. There had been loads of
berries here last week, plump, almost ripe, heavy enough
to bend the bushes down, but now Henry found only

a handful here and there. Sarah came out of the patch.

"You suppose Mr. Franklin picked them?" Henry asked her.

"I don't think so. It was probably someone from Wynnton." She seemed resigned to the loss, but Henry knew she had planned to make raspberry dumplings for supper.

"Is there anywhere else we could find some?" he asked.

Sarah thought for a moment, then said, "There might be some by the old Dunlap tipple, but it's too far."

"I'll go. How do I get there?"

"If you cut up over the hill there, you can't miss the gravel road. Just follow it to the tipple. But I warn you, it's a long walk."

"I've got all day." Henry grinned.

"Someone may have picked them, too, even though they are on my land," Sarah said.

"I may find some before I get to the tipple." Henry watched Sarah begin her descent to the house, then he climbed the hill and swung down the far side. The road was a tunnel of dark shade that he followed west, avoiding the gravel, walking instead along the road's edge in powdery dust that felt like velvet to his bare feet.

On a flat open stretch, he saw the tipple, the huge wooden structure that had screened the coal before it was loaded into trucks. The tipple had weathered to smoky gray, and there were so many boards missing that Henry was sure a man could walk up and push the whole thing over.

He scaled the rocky bank alongside the tipple, using the weeds to pull himself up, then crawled onto the level roadbed leading back to the mine entrance. There were lots of berries there and it took only minutes to fill the bucket.

Noticing the lengthening shadows, he realized he'd better get going if he hoped to have dumplings for supper. He slid down the bank and was about to start up the road again when he heard the sound of a motor. He thought of the timber thieves and wondered if they could be returning for more logs.

In an instant he faded into the tall weeds. From his hiding place he watched the vehicle slow, then pull off the road and crawl up the slope beside the tipple. If it was the thieves, maybe he could get a look at them. When the flat-bed lumber truck vanished over the crest of the hill, Henry set out after it.

He kept to the brush, moving slowly, for the sound of the motor had already died away. Either it was beyond hearing range or it had stopped. He paused to listen. The rumble of men's voices came from just ahead. The desire to see them, to see what they were doing, lured him on, even though his legs quivered and his breath came and went in short, uneven gulps.

He crept up a rise and settled down behind a fallen log. Below him sat the truck. Its original dark blue cab was now rusty brown, dented, and mud-spattered, with the running board on the passenger's side bent almost to the ground. A tall man, the stub of a cigarette hanging from his mouth, was unwinding a log chain from a winch on the truck bed while a smaller man pulled the chain away until he had gained enough slack to hook it around a log.

Henry had no trouble fixing the tall man's features in his memory: a ruddy, square-jawed face with a scarred eyebrow and a crumpled nose that must have been broken once. A long-billed cap hid the other man's face, but when he came toward the truck, Henry noticed that all four fingers were missing from his right hand. Only the thumb remained.

Wordlessly the men cranked the log toward the truck, then hauled it up the loading ramp and onto the truck bed. Then the tall man climbed into the truck, started the motor, and pulled ahead to another log. As the truck moved away, Henry saw the dog, a German shepherd, thick-bodied and shaggy, with its nose to the ground searching the underbrush. It stopped suddenly and looked up the rise, as if it sensed an alien presence.

Fearing the dog had caught his scent, Henry inched backward until he was sure he could not be seen. Then coming erect, he stole away through the woods, looking back over his shoulder to see if he was pursued. Each snap of a twig sounded like the crack of a rifle and Henry felt sure the dog heard and was on his trail. He broke into a run, fear driving him in such panic that he failed to see the fence until he was upon it.

He leaped into the air and cleared the top wire, but the

berry bucket went flying. He stopped just long enough to scoop up some of the berries, then took off again, this time running at full speed. The woods grew denser but still he ran, imagining he heard the dog barking and drawing ever nearer. When he tripped over a root and sprawled on his stomach, the last of the berries sprinkled down and were lost among the dead leaves.

He lay where he fell, lungs sobbing for air, ears straining for the certain sounds of pursuit. There was only the buzzing of the cicadas, the wind in the treetops, and from high overhead, the drone of a passing airplane. As his breathing slowed, he sat up and looked back the way he had come. The woodland was empty and still.

Tears began to run down Henry's face and, like a cleansing spring rain, washed away his terror. How foolish he had been to follow the truck. The empty berry bucket lay there as a reminder of his bad judgment. He'd walked all that way and picked the berries and now had nothing to show for his efforts. Even worse, he had no idea where he was. One thing was for certain: He'd better find his way back to civilization soon or he'd be spending the night in the woods.

It was after sunset but not yet full dark when he stumbled down a steep bank into a roadbed, deserted, but reassuring nevertheless. Following its winding way east, he had not gone far when the roadside trees gave way to fields, and he realized with surprise and relief that he was looking down the familiar valley. There was the Morrison place, just as he'd seen it when he first arrived. The house, though indistinct in the gathering night, was like an old friend.

Coming up the lane, he saw Sarah on the porch swing, her lips pursed in their usual indifference, while one hand stroked the kitten in her lap.

"I thought maybe you got lost," she said, eyeing the empty bucket.

"I did for a while," Henry replied. He hadn't realized how tired he was until he sank down on the steps. Then he told her about finding the berries, about the truck and the men and, of course, the dog.

"I think you'd better stay out of the woods. It's just too dangerous."

"I'm sorry about the berries. I had a whole bucketful," he said.

"We can get more berries," Sarah said, dismissing the loss with a wave of her hand. "You're probably hungry. I kept your supper on the back of the stove."

Henry followed her inside, not hurrying too much so that the kitten could slip through the door when he did. After a warm meal and a long, hot bath, Henry went to bed, leaving Sarah setting the kitchen in order and the kitten licking at a saucer of milk.

Even before he got out of bed the next morning, he could feel the soreness in his body. His legs hurt when he stretched and one shoulder was stiff. He thought back to the frantic flight through the woods. Driven by wild imaginings, he had run from a danger which had never materialized. In the morning light, it all seemed like a half-forgotten nightmare.

The kitten was a gray marble statue on the windowsill. Henry sat up and snapped his fingers, and it stretched with languid grace, then dropped to the floor and padded over to rub its cheek against his foot.

"You're a dandy," he whispered. "Say, that would be a good name for you . . . Dandy. Yep, that's what I'll call you."

When he stepped into the hall moments later, he met Sarah coming out of her room with an armload of clothes.

"Will you pull off your sheets and bring them down, Henry? I'm going to wash today." Henry nodded and turned back to his room to get them.

She must have been up early, for there was a roaring fire in the cookstove and steaming kettles of water on top. While she separated the clothes into piles on the kitchen floor, Henry ate breakfast, dropping a curl of bacon under his chair for Dandy when Sarah wasn't looking.

"I'll need some help when you get done," she said and went out.

Henry followed soon after and found her lifting the sloping cellar doors above a set of steep stone steps. Below, he paused to marvel at the great slabs of sandstone forming the basement walls. Even the floor was sandstone. He breathed in the mouth-watering aroma of apples and tangy vinegar.

They carried up the washtubs, one for washing and one for rinsing, along with the stools on which they would sit. Constructed of short vertical slats held together with iron bands, the tubs looked as though they were as old as the house, if not older.

After they had filled the tubs with hot water, Sarah brought out the washboard and soap, and when Henry offered to rinse, she shrugged a silent assent. He helped with the washing at home, not because he liked the work but because the job was just too much for one person with a family as big as theirs.

It was strange how little he thought of home these days. As he sloshed the clothes up and down, he remembered the day he'd first come to the Morrison place. How different Sarah seemed, now that he knew about her past. Perhaps she was just as preoccupied, but where the Sarah he'd first met had been a stranger, the present Sarah was a kind of hesitant friend.

When every inch of clothesline sagged with clean clothes, they draped the last few pieces on shrubs beside the house. Engrossed in emptying the tubs, they did not notice the truck backing into the lane until the door slammed. They turned just as a little man came into view. He was not much taller than Henry, with a stocky frame and muscled arms.

Henry stared at the truck bed protected by a wooden canopy and filled almost to the roof with boxes and cans. "It's Ed Doggleman," Sarah said to him. "He's a traveling grocer. Let's see what he has today."

As they walked toward the truck, the man greeted them with a smile. "Reckon you need anything today?" he asked Sarah. He tilted his head to one side and squinted at her.

"Yes," she replied, eyeing the jumbled wares. "Do you have any cinnamon?"

"Reckon I do." He knew exactly where to go for it and pulled out the small tin can. "Need any other spices? I got sage, nutmeg, cloves — "

"No, but I'll take three pounds of those dry beans."

Henry leaned around Sarah, examining the pantry on wheels which included some boxes of candy on a side shelf. Sarah spoke almost in his ear. "Henry, will you go in and get my purse out of the desk?" He nodded and loped away. When he returned, Sarah took out the familiar blue and red ration stamps, and she and the grocer haggled over them for several minutes before finally reaching agreement.

"These things are such a nuisance," Sarah said.

"Reckon so," the man replied, "but it's for the boys over there."

"You're right, Mr. Doggleman. The war seems far away if you don't have someone in it. Your boys joined the navy, didn't they?"

"Yep. Last we heard they were leaving San Francisco. We figure no news is goods news."

Sarah nodded, then turned to Henry and held out a nickel. Grinning his thanks, Henry took the coin. As she gathered up her purchases and went toward the house, he leaned into the truck. It was difficult to decide if the penny candies were a better buy than the smaller three-for-a-penny ones. Mr. Doggleman held a sack while Henry dropped in his selections.

"Reckon you're spending the summer with Miss Morrison."

"Yep," Henry said. "She needed help around here."

"Reckon she's a nice person to work for." The man made questions sound like statements, but Henry smiled at him. It was gratifying to hear someone say something favorable about Sarah.

"The place is looking better," the man said, gazing across the yard. "Reckon you been working hard."

Henry nodded and slipped a piece of candy into his mouth. Pushing it to one side, he said, "I've got some weeds to cut yet. Reckon they're not going anywhere." He and the traveling grocer grinned at each other.

Henry gave Mr. Doggleman his nickel. The man dropped it in his pocket, then lifted the tailgate and latched it. "Be seeing you around," he said, and went and slid under the wheel. "Much obliged," he called as he pulled away.

Henry popped another piece of candy into his mouth and sprinted up the lane. When he entered the kitchen, Sarah pointed to a brown paper package on the table.

"I got that for you."

Henry's mouth dropped open. She had bought something for him! Henry had received very few presents in his life, and never in the middle of summer before. People only gave presents when they had a reason, a birthday or Christmas. He stared at the package for several moments, his mind making guesses and rejecting them all.

"Open it," Sarah said.

Henry unwound the paper and found a hammer with a shiny steel head and claws and a smooth wooden handle. It was the first new tool he'd ever owned.

Sarah spoke from across the room. "I thought you could use a good hammer around here."

"This one's a dilly," Henry said, grinning at her, "but my birthday was in April."

A sudden strange light flared in Sarah's eyes. Henry thought at first it was fear, but that didn't make any sense. Whatever it was, it was gone in an instant, leaving her eyes veiled and distant once more. Maybe she wished she could take back the hammer. But when she turned away without a word, he figured she was probably just ill at ease giving presents. He wasn't very good at accepting them, either, because he hadn't even thanked her yet.

Tapping the hammer in his palm, he spoke to her rigid back. "Thanks a lot. I won't have to worry about this one coming off the handle."

Sarah was so busy at the stove she did not even acknowledge his thanks.

8
∎ ∎ ∎

In the middle of lunch the next day, Sarah jumped up and grabbed the broom from behind the stove, wielding it two-handed like a sword. "A mouse just ran under the icebox," she exclaimed. She crashed the broom to the floor, then flailed it again and again along the creature's wavering trail.

Henry saw the mouse run into a corner by the closed dining room door. "There it is." He pointed and Sarah came swinging, but missed again.

Just then Dandy flattened himself and peered under the icebox, stretching a curled paw into the darkness. The terrified animal dashed into the open again, but this time the kitten pounced on it, pinning it down with both paws. The mouse managed to wriggle free and ran across the braided rug by the stairs. Then, as if it realized it could not elude them forever, it stopped and huddled in surrender. Dandy sat down to watch it, but Sarah bore down on it with upraised broom.

"I'll get it," Henry said, dropping on all fours and scooping the mouse up in his hands. "If I put it out in the barn, it'll never find its way back here."

"That kitten's not much of a mouser," Sarah said, lowering her weapon.

"He just needs more practice," Henry said.

"Well, I can't wait for him to learn. I'm going to set some traps in here. I don't like animals in my kitchen."

Henry wondered if she were trying to tell him that she didn't want Dandy in the house, but when he returned from the barn, he saw the kitten crouched over a saucer of milk beside the stove.

Later, as he cut weeds along the lane, Henry saw where passing vehicles had thrown a lot of gravel over into the grass. He went for the rake and began working the gravel back into the roadbed. Sweat ran down into his eyes and a water blister rose in his right palm. Stopping to wipe his face, he caught sight of a horse coming up the road, head bobbing, harness clinking at every step. As it came nearer, he recognized the rider.

Evan walked the horse up to Henry and hooked a leg over the hames. "Whatcha doin'?"

"I'm raking the gravel out of the grass," Henry said.

"Looks like women's work to me."

"Well, it needs doin' so I'm doin' it," Henry said. How could a fellow be so consistently aggravating!

The horse stamped a front foot to rid himself of a biting fly, then blew out his breath through wet fluttering lips.

"Whoa, Mike." Evan yanked the reins and when the horse bobbed his head up and down to ease the painful bit, Evan pulled even harder.

"It's a nice horse," Henry said and stepped over to rub his fingers against the velvety nose.

"We're gonna work the corn. That oughta take some of the ginger out of him."

"I noticed the weeds were about as tall as the corn," Henry said.

"I just said we was gonna work it, didn't I?"

With a quick upward glance, Henry turned back to his raking and was relieved when he heard the horse clomping away. A few minutes later Earl Pickett pulled his truck into the field. Mary Beth slid out of the cab, gave Henry a wave, then went over to watch her father and Evan adjust the horse's harness. Henry did not look up again until he heard Pickett bellow. Turning, he saw Evan cowering against the horse's neck with hunched shoulders and bowed head, like a dog awaiting a thrashing.

Pickett stomped away from Evan and climbed into the truck. Mary Beth leaped onto the running board as the truck lurched backward, and by the time she had clambered inside the cab, they were headed down the valley, the wheels spraying gravel behind them. With one arm over the horse's neck, Evan kicked at the dry clods, sending up little explosions of dust.

Henry felt sorry for him. Never in his whole life had anyone screamed at Henry that way. He dropped the rake and tramped across the road. "You want to bring your horse over in the shade?" he asked the brooding boy.

Surprise flashed in Evan's face for only a moment,

then was gone. "Why don't you mind your own business!"

Henry shrugged his shoulders and started back across the road. He should've known better than to try to be nice to the fellow.

"Say, did you and old lady Morrison get some raspberries?" The smoothness in Evan's voice put Henry on guard.

"We haven't got any yet," he said.

"I thought you had a whole patch to yourself up there." Evan waved a hand toward the hilltop.

"We did, but somebody picked them."

"Is that right?" Evan said with exaggerated surprise that did not fool Henry for a minute.

Realizing the truth, he moved toward Evan, his fists clenching and unclenching. "You picked 'em, didn't you?" he said in a trembling voice.

When Evan saw him coming, he moved away from the horse, his arms curved out from his body. "Yeah. So?"

Henry's shoulders slumped and he felt the blood rush to his face. He was angry not only because Evan had picked the berries but also because Evan wanted to be sure that he knew it. "Sarah was looking forward to them berries," he said.

"Well, that's real sad, ain't it. It just so happens them berries ain't on her land."

"But Mr. Franklin lets her pick 'em every year." Henry knew he was wasting his time trying to reason with Evan.

"Yeah. Well, I figure, first come, first served."

"It's the same as stealing," Henry said.

"Are you callin' me a thief?" Evan rolled forward on his toes but Henry did not give an inch.

"Picking them berries wasn't right, and you know it." But there was nothing to be done about it now, Henry thought, and he turned away in disgust.

Evan grabbed his shoulder and pulled him around. "Say, ain't you a righteous Roy! You and old lady Morrison make a good pair."

"Don't you talk about her," Henry said.

"Are you defending that murderer?"

"You don't know the truth of it," Henry said softly.

"And I s'pose you know the whole story," Evan said.

For a moment Henry debated whether or not to tell Evan what he knew about Sarah. How could it hurt to tell the truth? Maybe then he'd stop calling her names.

"Sarah never murdered her baby. She gave it away 'cause her parents wouldn't let her keep it." For the first time since Henry had crossed the road, Evan had no retort. "A young couple who didn't have any children of their own took the baby," Henry continued. "So I wish you wouldn't tell them tales anymore."

"And where'd you git your facts?" Evan demanded.

"Willie told me and he knows 'cause he was here when it happened." Henry remembered Willie's plea not to talk about it. He'd broken a confidence, but someone had to set Evan straight. From the look on Evan's face, Henry knew he could not be trusted to let the story die.

"But she did have a baby without being married, didn't she?" When Henry nodded, Evan's mouth widened in a grin. "Then she's a whore, no matter what else she didn't do."

That was all Henry could take. He flung himself at Evan with all his strength. They both staggered backward, then fell to the ground. For several moments they rolled in the dirt, but Evan's weight gave him the advantage and he came out on top.

"What the hell's the matter with you?" he shouted. Then, as if in a hurry to get out of Henry's reach, he sprang to his feet, rubbing his hands against his thighs and watching Henry.

Henry rolled over on all fours and stood up on trembling legs. He steadied himself for a moment, then charged at Evan again. But this time Evan was on guard and his fist glanced off of Henry's nose, a blow solid enough to bring blood.

Though the punch slowed Henry, his momentum carried him against Evan and they sprawled on the ground a second time. Again Evan quickly overpowered him. "Why you standin' up for her? She's just a crabby old maid," he said. Despite his advantage, he slid off as soon as Henry ceased struggling.

Henry rose on one knee and swiped at his bleeding nose. If I did nothing else, he thought, at least I got rid of that stupid grin. When Henry finally got to his feet, Evan fell back a step, arms dangling at his sides. Henry faced him squarely and said, "You got no right to call her names."

Evan exhaled aloud, then jammed his hands into his pockets and crumbled a clod under his heel. "People always said — " he started, but Henry interrupted him.

"Do you believe everything you hear? She never did anything to you. What have you got against her?"

"She don't like me," Evan mumbled.

"That's no reason to tell lies about her."

"She does things for Mary Beth but she ain't never done nothing for me."

"Have you ever done anything for her?"

Evan stopped kicking at the dirt and looked at Henry.

"She's lived here all alone. Have you ever offered to help her with the work?" Again Evan had no answer.

"She's a good person, no matter what people say," and with that, Henry stalked away. It all seemed kind of silly now, he thought, as he headed back across the road. They had started out arguing over Evan picking the raspberries and ended up fighting over Sarah's past, neither of which could be undone.

Henry glanced toward the house but Sarah was nowhere in sight. He wished he could put some cold water on his throbbing nose, but he didn't want her to know he'd been fighting. She'd ask why and he couldn't tell her.

Henry was back at work when he heard the horse's hoofs in the gravel.

"I reckon Mike would be better off in the shade," Evan said.

Henry waved a hand toward the nearest maple and continued raking, trying to ignore the boy stretched out beside the grazing horse.

Henry finally finished his job. He had worked up a real thirst and was heading toward the kitchen to get a drink when Pickett's truck came barreling up the road.

Evan jumped to his feet, then stepped over to intercept Henry. "Anyway . . . there's some berries over there on the hill," he said, pointing to the pasture beyond the cornfield.

Henry turned and looked at the hillside, but before he could reply, Evan grabbed the horse's reins and went hurrying down the lane. It was probably just another of Evan's lies, Henry thought. But I'll walk up there in case, he decided, and if there aren't any berries, I'll never let on I went. He put the rake in the woodshed, then paused in the shade to watch Evan and his father lift the cultivator out of the truck and hitch the horse to it. Then Evan set off between the rows, the reins looped over one shoulder.

Henry stole up to the screen door and, finding the kitchen deserted, went inside and washed the blood from his hands, then splashed cold water on his face. He was drying off when Sarah came down the stairs. She went to the icebox and began setting out food for lunch.

They both turned at the knock on the door and saw Mary Beth peering through the screen. When Sarah invited the girl in, she slipped through the door, barefoot, wearing bib overalls, hair straggling across her face.

"Have you had lunch yet?" Sarah asked her.

"Nope. We didn't have time." A smile brightened her small round face when she looked at Henry.

"Sit here." Sarah motioned her to a chair at the table and as the girl slid into it, Sarah continued. "How about a slice of bread? I've been trying to get Henry to finish this loaf so I can bake some fresh." She cut a thick slice, spread butter on it, then handed it to Mary Beth. "Maybe it's too old already." She raised her eyebrows and waited for the girl to take a bite.

"Nope. It tastes good," Mary Beth said.

"Well, I'm glad to hear that. How's your knee?"

"It's all healed up," Mary Beth said around a mouthful of bread.

Henry sat and ate, a silent observer. He could see how Sarah's gentle attention made the girl bloom and, in return, brought a warmth to Sarah's face. They were good for each other, he concluded. He had not spoken to Mary Beth since their first meeting, yet he felt they were friends.

"I saw your dad leave a while ago in quite a hurry," he said. Mary Beth gazed at him with solemn eyes. "Evan forgot to put a singletree in the truck, so we had to go get it." Henry nodded and went on with his lunch. After the girl had eaten a chunk of cheese and a cold chicken leg, Sarah took her into the parlor.

Henry finished eating and went out on the porch. He sat down on the porch swing to watch the activity across the road. Evan was walking behind the two-handled cultivator, his eyes never straying from his narrow course between the knee-high rows of corn. At the end of the field he paused and slipped out of the reins, and his father took his place.

Evan lifted a bucket from the truck and came toward the house. "Can I git some water for the horse?" he asked, propping a foot on the bottom step. He pointed to the tabby kitten. "Where'd he come from?"

"Willie brought him to me last week."

"What do you call him?"

"Dandy," Henry replied. "I'll get your water." Evan handed him the bucket, then held out a coaxing hand to the kitten. When Henry came back with the water, he saw Evan holding Dandy upside down by his paws. The kitten was struggling to get free.

"Did you know a cat always lands on his feet?" Evan asked. Without warning, he let go of Dandy. The kitten fell, but before hitting the ground he righted himself and landed on all four feet. Evan snickered and scooped up the kitten again.

"Don't do that anymore."

Henry's tone made Evan look up. "It don't hurt 'em none," he declared.

"Just leave him alone," Henry said. "Here's your water," he added, setting down the bucket so solidly that water sloshed over the rim.

Evan shrugged. "Well, I didn't mean nothin' by it. It just always seemed funny to me that a cat can turn like that."

Henry picked up the kitten, cradled him in his arms, and sat down on the porch swing. Evan seemed in no hurry to get the water back to the field. He was still looking at the kitten in Henry's lap.

"You have a cat?" Henry asked him.

"Yeah, lots of 'em. They keep down the mice."

"Dandy cornered a mouse this morning, but he didn't know what to do with it." Henry couldn't help but grin when he remembered the kitten's friendly curiosity.

"Oh, he'll learn. He's young yet." How strange that sounded coming from Evan, Henry thought, a statement devoid of boasting or belligerence. "Say, I'm s'posed to work for Franklin tomorrow puttin' up hay. You could probably work, too, if you wanted to."

"I'm getting paid to work for Sarah," Henry said.

"Well, I just thought if she'd give you a day off, you could make some extra money. 'Course, you couldn't do as much as me, but he'd pay you something."

Henry almost smiled. Now, that sounded like the real Evan. "I don't think I can," Henry said.

Evan shrugged his shoulders, picked up the bucket of water, and headed down the lane.

A little while later Mary Beth stepped out on the porch, followed by Sarah. The girl's hair, half covering her face before, was now held high on her crown with a white pearl barrette, exposing her dainty features to the sun. She gave Henry a passing smile and took off for the cornfield with a swinging stride.

Henry and Sarah watched as Mary Beth approached her father. She touched the barrette and Henry could imagine she was saying, "Ain't it pretty?" Pickett stared down at the girl for a moment, then reached out and snatched the barrette from her hair without even unclasping it. He thrust it into Mary Beth's hand and shoved her toward the road. Henry could not distinguish any words, but Pickett's rage was unmistakable.

With slow steps, Mary Beth returned to the porch. "My dad says to give this back," she said, handing the barrette to Sarah. Henry expected to see tears, but the girl apparently was used to her father's wrath.

The anger in Sarah's face was quite plain, but controlled. "I gave this to you, Mary Beth, and as far as I'm concerned, it's still yours. I'll just keep it for you until you're allowed to have it."

She reached out and brushed back the girl's straggling hair. Mary Beth smiled up at her, then turned and trod slowly down the lane, her thin shoulders squared as she walked toward her father.

In late afternoon the Picketts finished their work and departed, the truck first, then Evan astride the plodding horse. Their day's labor left the field of corn bright green against the dark worked earth.

Henry could finally see some results from his own work. Most of the tall weeds around the house had been cut, and there was a clear, wide path to Sarah's garden. Sometime soon they would burn the brush pile and finish cleaning up the lot behind the chicken house. Sarah was right; a farm needed a family to work it.

Remembering the berries Evan had told him about, Henry went inside for a bucket. He stopped to watch Sarah cutting thin yellow strips of noodles from the dough rolled out on the floured tabletop. Every so often she paused, picked up a handful, and shook them into loose ringlets.

"Evan says there's some berries on the hill across the road," Henry said. "I'm going up to see."

Once out of the cornfield, he waded through waist-high weeds, using his bucket to push aside the briars. He was halfway up the hillside before he found the berry bushes, but sure enough, their long arching branches were loaded with berries. Evan had told the truth! In no time Henry had his bucket filled.

He lingered there in the sun, gazing across the valley where the Morrison farm backed up against the dark woods. The place looked better with some of the weeds gone. And even though it was run down, it was a nice place to live.

Three generations of Morrisons had called the farm their home. Now it was Sarah's home, although she said she would be the last. Henry had never thought much about the meaning of home. It was simply the place he happened to be. Gorleyville was home, Grandma's farm was home, and he guessed the Morrison place was home now, at least for the summer.

He tried to imagine the farm blanketed in dazzling winter snow. It was impossible when there before him were the sun-bleached outbuildings, the bright rows of vegetables and flowers in Sarah's garden, the emerald-leafed maples that sheltered the graying house.

The vibrant colors made Henry feel warm inside, the way he felt sometimes when he saw a rainbow arcing across the sky. He was almost glad he would not be there in the fall to see the flowers die and the leaves fall. He wanted to remember the Morrison place as it was now, homey and inviting and bright with the colors of summer.

9
...

"Henry!" Sarah's voice invaded his sleep. "Henry, Evan is here!" The insistent tone told him she would not be put off. He opened his eyes and saw her leaning through the doorway. "They need help with the haying today. Can you come down and talk to him?"

Henry nodded and propped himself up on one elbow. "I'll tell him you're coming," Sarah said and disappeared.

Henry got up and rubbed his eyes, then walked over to the window. Bold shadows slanting away from the barn told him it was still early in the day, but he could already feel the heat building.

Downstairs, he spied Evan on the porch, gazing down the valley. He walked to the screen door. "I told you the other day that I couldn't work."

At his words Evan spun around. "But Franklin sent me. He needs another man real bad."

"Maybe you'd better go, Henry," Sarah broke in. "That hay is pretty important to Mr. Franklin."

Henry did not relish the idea of spending the whole day with Evan. "Well, I didn't think I should, since I'm supposed to be working here."

"There's nothing to do here today that won't wait. I think you ought to go." Henry looked from her to Evan, then nodded. Sarah turned to the stove and began hurrying breakfast.

As soon as Henry had eaten, he and Evan set off down the road. Evan led the way, talking little, until they climbed the fence into Franklin's pasture field. Then he stepped over and let Henry come alongside.

"I'm gonna buy Mom a present with the money I make today," Evan said. "Her birthday's week after next." When Henry nodded, Evan continued. "She never gits anything nice. S'pose she'd like some perfume?"

"I guess so," Henry said.

They walked on in silence to the sun-baked hay field. The hay, raked into windrows, lay in long brown stripes across the stubbled field. Two flat wagons stood under a nearby tree, the two teams of horses hitched and ready.

Franklin, checking a team's harness, greeted the boys with a smile. "Glad you could come, Henry. You boys'll be up on the wagons."

Henry nodded. He knew what was expected. He would tramp down the hay forked up to him, designing a load that would stay on the wagon for the trip back to the barn.

A lanky young man came over and stood wiping his face, studying Henry from under thick black eyebrows.

"Henry, this is Wayne Burkey," said Mr. Franklin. "He'll be pitching the hay to you."

"Howdy," Wayne said. "This is my wagon." He pointed to the nearest one. "You look a mite small . . . ." His eyes twinkled. "But I reckon we'll get our share into the barn." Henry grinned and hopped up on the wagon. He untied the reins and looked around for directions.

Wayne was already swinging toward the first windrow with a pitchfork on one shoulder. "Pull 'em up, partner," he shouted.

Henry rippled the lines along the horses' backs and the wagon started with a jerk. Wayne opened up the windrow, then began pitching hay on the wagon, trusting Henry to put it in the right place.

Henry tramped back and forth, pushing the hay toward the outer edge with his pitchfork. The work was easy at first. But when the wagon bed was covered and the load began to rise, Henry had to lift his knees almost to his chin to get on top of the hay. Every forkful showered him with dust and seeds and brittle grass. His head and arms and back itched, his eyes burned from the dust, and his sweaty clothes clung to him. The only rest he got was the brief ride from one windrow to the next. At those times he looked to the other side of the field where Evan's load was taking shape, high and solid and neat.

Finally, when Henry's load rose so high that Wayne could no longer reach the top, Wayne leaned on his pitchfork, looked up at Henry, and said, "I believe we've got enough." Flashing a quick grin, he stepped on the wagon tongue and climbed up beside Henry. "Let's head for the barn," he said, falling back flat on the hay.

Henry let the horses pick their way across the field and along the dirt road. Though the load of hay lurched from side to side over the uneven ground, none of it fell off.

Wayne pointed to a buzzard circling overhead. "He's looking for something to eat," he said. "You ever shoot a buzzard?"

"Nope," Henry replied. "I never shot anything, not even a rabbit."

"I guess we're lucky we don't have to shoot people . . . like they're doing over in Europe." Wayne paused, then went on. "I should be over there, you know."

"In the war?" Henry asked.

"Yeah. Everybody around here's gone but me."

"Why didn't you go?" He hoped Wayne wouldn't think he was too nosey.

"Because I was deferred. They thought I could do more good farming. All the other fellows are seeing the world while I'm stuck here at home."

"At least you don't get shot at back here," Henry said. "A war isn't a very safe place."

"No, but it's exciting," Wayne said. "I got a letter from a buddy of mine, and he said a bullet bounced right off his helmet. He heard it ping."

"You're lucky you got deferred," Henry said, grinning.

"I don't know. People think I'm a coward. I'm not afraid to go, but everyone thinks I just used the farm to get out of going. They figured I stayed home because I wanted to. Well, one day the war will be over and those guys will be back here pitching hay, too."

They rode the rest of the way in silence, until Henry pulled the team to a stop behind Evan's wagon, already in place for unloading. Using a two-pronged hay fork connected to the roof by a series of ropes and pulleys, Wayne and Mr. Franklin lifted the hay into the barn. Up in the haymow Evan and Henry leveled each pile as it dropped, sweltering in the hot air trapped beneath the tin roof.

When both loads had been stored away, the boys climbed down the ladder into the ground floor coolness. Mrs. Franklin, a rail-thin woman with a braid of wispy hair wound around her head, met them with a pitcher of lemonade and glasses. "They gave you boys the hard job, didn't they?" she remarked as she poured.

Henry thought the ice clinking against glass was the most beautiful sound he had ever heard. After drinking in long noisy gulps, he and Evan held out their glasses for a refill, then followed Mrs. Franklin outside. The hay wagons stood in the shade, the horses still hitched to them, loosened reins letting their noses reach the ground. The horses grazed contentedly, sometimes inching the wagons forward to reach a choice clump of grass.

After a brief rest, the haymakers headed for the field again. Once the second loads were stowed away, Mrs. Franklin called them to a table in the yard for a dinner of fried chicken, mashed potatoes with thick brown gravy, noodles, peas, fresh-baked rolls, and sweet pickles. When Henry was sure he could not eat another bite, she brought out a frosty canister of homemade vanilla ice cream.

Under a waning sun, they mounted the wagons again and crossed the railroad. This field was smaller than the first, but they still got two full wagons of hay. As Henry and Evan headed for the haymow, Mr. Franklin stopped them. "No need for you boys to go up there again. We'll just drop it in and let it lay."

After the hay was unloaded, Wayne climbed up on his wagon and prepared to go home. "See you, partner." He waved to Henry. "You may be a little fella, but you got a heart for work."

Mr. Franklin lifted his hand and said, "Much obliged, Wayne. Let me know when your hay is ready."

"I will. You suppose we can persuade these fellas to help us again?"

"Could be." Franklin turned to Henry and Evan. "You boys think you might want another haying job?"

"I'm ready anytime," Evan said.

"I'd have to ask Miss Morrison," Henry said, "but I'd be willing."

Wayne nodded to them and made a kissing noise to his horses, and the wagon rattled off down the road.

"Well," Franklin sighed, "if I had my cows milked, I could call it a day. Oh, I reckon you boys want to be paid. I'll be back in a minute." He crossed the yard with lagging steps and entered the house.

"I wonder how many cows he milks," Henry said.

"Somewhere around twenty," Evan said. "His wife helps since Lyle went to the war."

"You think we ought to stay and help him?" Henry asked.

"Heck no! I done my day's work. I'm goin' home soon as I git paid."

Mr Franklin came toward them carrying a milk bucket in one hand and two bills in the other.

"I'm giving you boys five dollars apiece for the good day's work you did. And I'm much obliged."

Henry had never earned that much money in one day. He folded the bill several times and pushed it down to the bottom of his pants pocket. "Thanks a lot, Mr. Franklin," he said.

"Yeah, thanks," Evan said.

"You're both welcome. I'm mighty glad to get that hay in," Franklin said, turning toward the barn.

"I could stay and help you with the milking," Henry offered.

Mr. Franklin turned back to him with a smile. "That's real neighborly," he said.

Evan stepped forward. "I'll help too. Ain't nobody lookin' for me home yet."

While Henry was milking one of the docile Guernseys, his legs grew as heavy as logs, and he leaned forward until his head rested against the cow's solid warm flank. It had been a long day. Then like a soft dream, he heard singing, clear, melodious. It was Evan. "There's a long, long trail a windin' . . ." Who would have thought Evan could sing like that!

Abruptly the singing stopped and Evan walked by with a bucket of milk. He returned and sat down to milk again, his rhythmic strokes keeping time with his soothing song. "From this valley they say you are goin' . . ." Henry hummed along, but softly so that Evan wouldn't hear him.

After Evan's song ended, Mr. Franklin called out, "When you boys finish with those cows, you'd better get on home. It's almost dark."

Henry carried his almost-full bucket of milk into the milk house and turned it over to Mrs. Franklin.

"You've been a mighty big help," she said. "Sarah's lucky to have such a good worker. You going to stay all summer?"

"Yep. Till school starts."

"Well, we'll see more of you then. Stop in anytime."

"I will," Henry promised. Just then Evan came in with his frothy bucket of milk.

"After that long day's work, you can still sing?" Mrs. Franklin asked him.

"Yeah . . . singin' and milkin' sorta go hand-in-hand."

Henry and Evan walked out to the road together, slowing to a stop as they came to the crossroads.

"Did you find them berries?" Evan asked.

"Yep. I got a whole bucketful. Sarah made dumplings with 'em." Henry bent down and pulled at a piece of trouser leg that had torn loose and now caught under his foot at every step. He ripped it as far as the seam but it wouldn't let go.

"Wait a minute," Evan said. He reached into his pocket, pulled out a penknife, and opened it before handing it to Henry. "Don't you have a knife?"

"Nope," Henry said, sawing through the seam. He tossed the strip away, then folded up the blade and held the knife out to Evan.

"Just keep it," Evan said, turning away in the direction of home.

"But you'll need it."

"Naw ... I got another one at home." Evan walked down the road a little way, then looked back at Henry. "I'll be seein' you."

"Yep. Thanks for the knife," Henry called. "And thanks for the berries, too," he added. But Evan was already some distance down the road, hands in his pockets, fading into the darkness.

10

...

In midmorning of a clear, dazzling day Henry swung up the road, heading for Willie's house. Willie had told them he had lots of berries and they could pick all they wanted. Henry had gladly volunteered for the task.

In his berry bucket, Henry carried a load of Sarah's fresh-baked bread. She's kind, he thought, but she must get lonesome, keeping to herself the way she does. If people would only get to know her, they'd like her, even though she does act unfriendly sometimes.

Following Sarah's directions, Henry turned into the narrow road leading to Willie's house. He found some berries and picked along, eating as many as he put in his bucket. The trees gradually closed overhead until he walked in deep, cool shade. Then around a curve he spied the log house. Firewood stacked from floor to roof filled one end of the front porch, and in the lone rocking chair a ginger cat lay curled asleep. "Hello," Henry called toward the house, then held his breath, listening.

"I'm back here," came the faint reply.

As Henry rounded the corner of the house, he saw Willie at the edge of the woods. "Just stay there," Willie called. "I got these bees all stirred up." A ragged piece of curtain hung from the man's straw hat and down over his shoulders. Henry watched him lift a thin wooden platform from the hive, then replace the lid.

Coming across the field, Willie removed the hat and veil. "Just stealing a little honey," he said. Brushing off a golden honeybee, he held out the frame to Henry. "Want a taste?"

Henry dipped his finger into the honey, then at Willie's urging broke off a piece of the honeycomb and popped it into his mouth. He chewed until all the sweetness was gone, leaving only a tasteless lump of wax.

In the kitchen Willie scraped the honeycomb from the frame onto a large platter, then took a quart jar from the cupboard and filled it with honey-laden comb. He set the jar on the table beside Henry. "Now, you take that home with you," he said. After rinsing the stickiness off his hands, he faced Henry. "You came after berries, I reckon."

"Sarah said you've got more than you need," Henry said, setting the loaf of homemade bread on the table.

Willie grinned. "Come and see for yourself."

Henry followed him along a well-worn path to the berry patch. "It shouldn't take you long to fill your bucket," said Willie. "When you're finished, stop by the house. We'll have a bite to eat."

Henry left the patch a short while later with the bucket so full that despite his careful handling, berries kept jiggling out. "Sarah's going to make jelly," he told Willie when he reached the back porch.

"I've tasted Sarah's jelly. It's blue-ribbon. Say, how's the tabby doing? Catching any mice?"

"He had one cornered the other day, but he didn't know what to do with it. I caught it and took it to the barn." He grinned at Willie.

While Henry went to the springhouse for a jug of milk, Willie made them each a fried egg sandwich. Several cats padded in through the open doorway and begged for food until finally Willie poured milk into a saucer and set it on the floor. The cats crowded around it, lapping quietly.

"Where'd you serve in the army?" Henry asked when he'd finished eating. He'd been saving up questions to ask Willie about his army career.

"Well, I've been all over this country of ours. Then I traveled around the Mediterranean . . . went to North Africa for a few months. And I spent some time in the Philippines. You know where the Philippines are, Henry?"

"Yep. We studied them in school."

"I liked the people, the land. . . . I still have a coconut I brought home from Luzon. . . . Come in here."

Henry followed him into a long room that stretched across the front of the house. There was a rough stone fireplace at the far end, a set of deer antlers over the mantel, a tabby cat sleeping on the hearth beside a bowl of leftover popcorn. Willie took the coconut from a shelf, dusted it off, and passed it to Henry. Then he went back to the bookcase for a big, untidy scrapbook.

"I've collected a lot of souvenirs over the years," he

said, settling down on the sofa, patting the cushion for Henry to join him. They sat with the book across their laps, studying the pictures and mementos from distant lands. Henry lost all track of time. Fading photographs of Willie with other men, all in their uniforms, a coffee-stained napkin with strange markings, a square cloth patch divided into three vivid colors with a gold sword embossed over it — all told of sojourns in faraway places. Willie had something fascinating to say about every item.

He picked up a crinkled snapshot and handed it to Henry. A young soldier and two small Oriental boys posed beside a mud-caked army tank. One boy held a black and white puppy in his arms.

"That's a friend of mine. . . . He's in the Pacific right now," Willie said. "Some strange things happen in war. Those two boys and their pup survived a Japanese attack, but everyone else in their family was killed." Henry gazed at the dirty, ragged boys, seeing in their haggard faces and haunted eyes the terrible hurt of war. "I hope you never have to go to war, Henry."

"I hope so too. I don't want to get killed, and I don't want to kill anybody either."

"It seems like the children suffer the most during war," Willie said, gently placing the picture back in the album.

Henry's mind came spinning back from the war on the other side of the world. He was thinking of Sarah's child. "You never said if Sarah's child was a boy or a girl."

It took Willie a little longer to return to the present. "It was a boy," he said. "I remember clearly that spring he was born. I was just getting this place cleaned up after a long winter. Back toward the quarry I found a pair of hawks shot, and a baby left in the nest."

Willie began gathering up the souvenirs and returning them to the overcrowded album. "I adopted the ugly little fellow and kept him until the following spring. Then I set him free. A couple of weeks later I found him shot, too. That's when I decided something had to be done about the hawks."

If Sarah's son was born in 1930, Henry calculated, he would be my age. At least she doesn't have to worry about him going off to war. Henry wondered if she ever thought of her son and wished she had not given him away.

"Sarah told me last week she's pleased with your work," Willie said. "Maybe she's beginning to wonder what she missed, not having a family. Well, she may have one yet," he finished.

"No, she won't. She said she's never getting married. She doesn't like kids, especially boys."

"Whatever gave you that idea?" Willie said. "She likes you. She said when she saw you and Evan fighting that — "

"She saw that? But she never said anything."

"She didn't know what you were fighting about, but she told me you held you own." Henry blushed, remembering that he had been the only one with a bloody nose.

"Sarah thinks a lot of you, Henry. If she seems cool toward you, it's just because she's afraid to care, afraid she'll be hurt again."

"I wouldn't hurt her," Henry said. "That's why I was fighting Evan. He called her a bad name."

"Names can't hurt Sarah anymore," Willie said. "It's the loss of her child that grieves her. And knowing that her son may be lonely and longing for the mother he never knew."

It was on the long walk back to the Morrison place that the thought came to Henry, a vague, unsettling idea that sharpened into a deep, throbbing knot in his stomach. He slumped down beside the road. It couldn't be! Things like that didn't happen, except in fairy tales. He sat there, muttering, rolling a piece of gravel between his palms, until he thought he had talked himself out of the idea that he was Sarah's son.

If the baby had been given to a young couple, as Willie had said, then he was probably still living with them. "I'm not her son," he said aloud, knowing how ridiculous it was even to think such a thing. Besides, he told himself, he had no desire to be that abandoned boy. But once the theory had taken shape, his mind would not let go of it, and by the time he reached the Morrison place, the gossamer daydream had evolved into a fragile possibility.

Sarah was sitting on the porch swing, not swinging, just sitting there with the kitten in her lap. Henry did not look at her as he set down the jar of honey and the bucket of berries. He was afraid she might see into his mind, as she sometimes seemed to do.

"That looks good." Sarah stood up, came over, and

picked up the jar. "And I see I'll be in the jelly business tomorrow."

Henry braced himself and looked up. "I'm going up to bed," he said.

"Aren't you feeling well?" she asked, following him through the screen door.

"I'm just tired."

Sarah stopped by the stove. "I'll fry you a couple of eggs, if you're hungry."

"No, I ate with Willie," he said, trying not to hurry to the stair door. All he wanted was the sanctuary of his room.

Once there, he closed the door and went to the window to watch darkness creeping out of the woods and across the garden. When he heard Dandy in the hall, he opened the door to let him in, then undressed and climbed into bed. But sleep was far away. He lay on his back, hands under his head, gazing out at the darkening sky. His mind worried and gnawed at the idea of being Sarah's son. At the same time he knew that even if it might be true, she would never let him be a Morrison. She would not take back the son she'd given away all those years ago.

When he drifted off to sleep at last, Henry dreamed a dreadful dream in which he sought out Sarah in the basement and confronted her with the staggering idea. "You're my mother; I know you are."

"Oh, Henry, how absurd! I'm not your mother. Your mother ran off with a railroad engineer."

"You are my mother," Henry insisted. He even went

so far as to stamp his foot on the damp stone floor.

"No, Henry," Sarah lowered her voice and slowly shook her head. "Don't you remember? I killed my baby."

Henry lunged up the basement steps, dropped the slanted wood doors, then began nailing them shut. There, that would fix her!

The nightmare sound of hammer against nail jerked him awake, and he lay shivering in his own cold sweat. He sprang out of the bed as if it were full of hot coals. Dressing in seconds, he tiptoed down the steps, pausing at the bottom to listen. The only sound was Dandy's feather-light footsteps on the stairs. Sarah wasn't up yet.

"You have to stay," he whispered, rubbing the kitten's ears. He had to get away from this place, get out in the woods where he could think things through. He just couldn't face Sarah this morning, not when his mind fluttered with the scary, wonderful idea that she might be his mother.

He went to the icebox and took out a slice of meat loaf, then tore a chunk of bread from the brown loaf in the cupboard. Slipping outside, he sprinted for the woods. Once in the shelter of the trees, he turned to stare at the hulking farmhouse and watched the climbing sun dust the roof with gold. A lump rose in Henry's throat and he turned into the deep green woods.

Walking, nibbling at the meat loaf sandwich, he wrestled with the incredible idea. Could he be Sarah's son? If he really was, wouldn't he know it, feel it somehow? When he tried to picture Sarah as a mother, the familiar image of her, aloof, impassive, with her strange solitary ways, rose strong and clear in his mind. She seemed so uncaring. But then, he reasoned, she'd never had any practice at being a mother.

The possibility of having a real mother somewhere had never seemed important to Henry until this spring, when Mrs. Compton became so cool and began pushing him to the edge of the family. First she'd sent him over to eat with old Mrs. Kohler one night a week. Then she'd arranged for him to do odd jobs around Lavertine's store in exchange for a haircut so that she wouldn't have to cut his hair herself. Finally she'd found Henry this summer job.

Maybe he was just looking for someone to care a little more about him. Sarah had let him have the kitten, and she'd given him the hammer for no reason at all. Then yesterday Willie had said she liked Henry. But none of that meant she was his mother. And being born in the same year as Sarah's baby didn't prove anything. There were lots of boys born in the spring of 1930. Why should he be that special one, that child Sarah had given away?

Henry rambled through the woods, tramping out the last sparks of his foolish daydream. It was best to leave things as they were. A fellow could get along without a mother; he'd been doing it for quite some time. Besides, he didn't know how to be Sarah's son any more than she knew how to be his mother. They were better off just friends.

As Henry walked along and thought of the long golden days stretching ahead to the end of summer, he felt almost happy. This was a good place to spend the summer, and Sarah really did need him. It was nice to be needed. He turned back toward the farm, determined that he was going to be a better friend to Sarah; she had so few.

When he stepped out of the woods, he was surprised to see the sun so far to the west. Nearing the house, he saw Dandy come padding down the steps, but Henry hurried past him to read the note attached to the screen door with a straight pin. In neat, rounded letters Sarah had written, *Come to Franklin's.* That was all; no names, no explanation, only that brief blunt command. She must have been in a hurry, to leave Dandy outside.

Henry tore the paper away and stuffed it in his pocket, then opened the door and pushed Dandy inside. He hurried down the lane and out into the road, running a few steps, then settling down to a rapid walk. Sarah never went to visit any of her neighbors. What could have lured her away from home? There was a tight knot in Henry's stomach by the time Franklin's house came into view.

11
▪ ▪ ▪

T here were cars parked along the road and men
loitering by the back porch, talking in low, guarded
tones. Inside the house shadowy figures moved back and
forth across the kitchen window. Henry saw Mary Beth
slip out through the screen door and close it carefully
behind her. When she saw Henry, she hurried toward
him, hands jammed into her overall pockets.

"What is it?" Henry wasn't sure why he whispered.

"Lyle Franklin's dead. They just got word today."

Henry's jaws clamped shut. He didn't know Lyle, but
he knew something about the leaden reality of death.
How could he ever forget that gray winter day when he
learned that his father had died!

"He got shot by the Germans. In Africa," Mary Beth
said.

"Is Sarah in the house?"

"Yeah. The women's fixin' supper."

"She wanted me to come down here. I reckon I ought
to let her know I'm here."

"There she is." Mary Beth pointed toward the house.
Sarah had come through the door, and when she saw

Henry she strode across the yard, a tight, dull expression on her face.

"I'm glad you're here, Henry. I told Mr. Franklin you'd help with the milking. Mrs. Franklin's just not up to it." Henry nodded. He was glad to have something to do besides just stand around.

"Mary Beth, I have a chore for you inside," Sarah said as she turned back toward the house.

Mary Beth ran to catch up with her, but all at once came sprinting back to Henry. "Sarah says you'll have supper here when you're done."

When Henry entered the barn, the cows were already in their stanchions, tails switching, trusting eyes following Mr. Franklin.

"I come to help you milk," Henry said.

The man's haunted eyes sought out Henry. "There's a bucket over there," he said.

Beginning with a cow he'd milked the day of the haying, Henry worked his way down the line. He could hear Mr. Franklin on the far side of the barn, rattling a bucket, his hand slapping a cow's flank. He jumped when the man appeared noiselessly beside him.

"Guess you heard about my boy." Henry swallowed hard before nodding. "He liked milking. Said it was a satisfying time for man and beast."

Mr. Franklin patted the cow next to Henry. "Move over, Tango." After he got started milking, he spoke again. "I wanted him to stay home. I could've got him deferred, but he wanted to go."

106·

Henry had no ready reply. What could he say? A boy couldn't console a man.

Returning from the milk house a little later, Henry noticed Mr. Franklin hammering at a loose door hinge. He dropped the hammer to his side and gazed out across the pasture. Then suddenly he lifted the hammer and struck the solid squared timber, again and again, and with each blow he uttered a terrible moan. Henry was afraid to move for fear the man would turn on him.

The hammer strokes stopped as abruptly as they had started, and Mr. Franklin sagged forward until his head rested against the battered timber. He remained there for a long time, then at last straightened up and saw Henry. "This farm was for him," he said. "Now what do I do with it?"

Because Henry could not begin to answer that question, he concentrated on the work at hand. "I guess the cows can be let out now," he suggested.

"He has such a love for the land ... had such a ..." Mr. Franklin's voice died away.

"You want the cows in the back pasture?" Henry asked.

"He tried to build up the soil, make this the best farm in the valley; even wanted to get more cows."

Not knowing what to do, Henry settled down beside the feed box, hugged his knees to his chest, and waited. Mr. Franklin turned the hammer slowly around in his hands and began talking, sometimes looking out the barn door, sometimes looking at Henry. His words were scraps of memory, trivial incidents, puzzling and incomplete, a rambling account of a family's life. At last he stopped and gazed out on a land hushed with twilight. Turning to Henry, he said, "Let's put the cows in the back pasture, Henry."

Even with all the bustle, the house had a subdued air and a kind of watchfulness, like a Sunday morning church just before the minister rises to speak. Henry caught Sarah's glance and her silent signal to come to the kitchen table.

"You can eat here," she said and began filling a plate from the numerous pots on the stove.

Mary Beth came over and sat down beside him. "Ain't them good peas?" she whispered.

"The chicken's good too," Henry replied, biting into his third chicken leg. People moved back and forth between the kitchen and the living room, treading softly.

"Mrs. Franklin's showin' Lyle's baby pictures," Mary Beth said. "Lyle gave me a quarter once. I bought a star for our Christmas tree, but we didn't git no tree that year."

They both turned as Mrs. Franklin came into the kitchen. Her eyes took in the quiet women at work, yet seemed to look through them. At the sink she filled a glass with water, then stared out the window without drinking. Sarah went to her and said something in a low voice. Tears glistened on the older woman's cheeks, but oddly, she smiled at Sarah. Her lips formed words Henry could read but not hear: "Thanks for coming."

The women's hands met and clasped, then Sarah turned and came over to Henry. "We'll go now."

Henry slid out of his chair and followed her out the door, lifting a farewell hand to Mary Beth.

They walked along in silence until Sarah breathed a long sigh. When she spoke, her voice was flat and tired. "I hope you never have to go to war, Henry."

"I hope so too," he replied, remembering that Willie had said the very same thing.

"Old men start wars and young men have to fight them." She sighed again. "No mother should have to bury her own child."

Henry thought of the Filipino boys who had lost everyone and had only each other and a pup. No little child should have to bury his father and mother, either. He was deep in these thoughts when the sound of a car made him jump to the side of the road. The vehicle swept by them and disappeared around a curve in the road, churning up a cloud of dust that left him and Sarah with gritty eyes and dry, crusty lips.

In the lane, Sarah spoke again. "I'm going to bake pies fist thing in the morning, and you can take them down to the Franklins'."

"When will he . . . When will they have the funeral?" Henry asked.

"The body won't get here for some time, maybe weeks

. . ." Sarah's voice faltered, and Henry did not dare look at her.

After she went into the house, Henry picked up an armload of firewood and took it inside. He had just dropped the load in the wood box when he saw a car pulling into the lane. A tall man came up to the porch, limping slightly. Henry noticed at once the silver star pinned to his shirt.

The man glimpsed Sarah through the screen door, propped a foot on the bottom step, and asked, "Is this the Morrison place?"

"Yes, I'm Sarah Morrison," she said, stepping outside. Henry followed her through the door.

The man turned to him. "Then you must be Henry Compton."

"Yep," Henry said, his heart pounding. How did this lawman know his name?

The man smiled as if he read Henry's thoughts. "Willie gave me your name. I passed you folks earlier on the road. Someone saw the timber thieves over on Wilson Ridge, but they were gone when I got there." The man hitched up the holster at his waist. "My name's Dan Warfield. I'd like to know what you saw that day in the woods, Henry."

"Won't you come up on the porch, Sheriff?" Sarah said.

"I'm not a sheriff, ma'am. I'm just a deputy." He smiled at Sarah, and for a moment Henry saw him as a mere man instead of a lawman.

"The invitation still stands, Mr. Warfield."

"I wish you'd call me Dan." He removed his hat and

dropped down on the top step, resting his back against the porch post. A chain squeaked as Sarah sat down on the swing.

"Did you get a look at the men?" Dan asked Henry.

"Yep," Henry said, then went on to describe what he had seen, including the truck and the dog. He refrained, though, from telling all of it, in particular his wild flight through the woods.

"Would you recognize the two again?" Dan asked.

"I reckon I would."

"You're the only one who's gotten a good look at them," Dan said. "So you be real careful in the woods. These men could be dangerous."

"I'll stay clear of them," Henry promised, thinking that the dog was even scarier than the men.

As they talked, night crept up the valley, and the kitchen lamp seemed to glow brighter minute by minute. The deputy shifted slightly and straightened out one leg.

"Have you been a deputy long?" Sarah asked.

"Less than a year. I was in the navy till the attack on Pearl Harbor. I almost lost a leg there. It still doesn't work too well." He grinned and rubbed the outstretched leg.

Henry stared, hardly able to believe that this man had been there during the attack and lived through it. "Did you see the planes dropping bombs?" he asked.

"Yes, I did, and it was a sight I never want to see again. The ships . . . all those men . . ." Dan stopped and shook his head.

Henry remembered Lyle Franklin, and the war didn't

sound as exciting as he had thought it would. He closed his eyes and tried to imagine the terrifying noise of bombs exploding, but all he heard was a calf bawling in the distance and a whippoorwill calling from the edge of the woods.

"Well, I'd better get going," Dan said, "but I'll be back this way. We'll get lucky one of these days and catch those fellows."

The next day, as Henry went toward Franklin's with the hot apple pies, he saw a truck coming up the valley road, a long cloud of dust spewing out behind it. Henry tucked the towel tighter around the pies and climbed up on the bank to let the vehicle pass. He recognized the truck long before he could see Pickett behind the wheel. Someone was with Pickett, but Henry was watching Pickett's face, wary of him and a little afraid.

The truck slid to a stop. Pickett leaned over his passenger and called through the open window, "What you got there, boy?"

"Pies for the Franklins," Henry began. "They — "

"Yeah, I heard. Say, I'll give you a quarter for one."

"Nope," Henry declared quickly. "Sarah made 'em for the — "

"She don't have to know. How about fifty cents?"

Henry shook his head, then glanced at the fence next to him. It would be some trick getting through that barbed wire with a basket of pies.

"Aw, what the hell! I didn't want one anyway," Pickett muttered. As he reached for the gearshift, he said something to the other man and they both laughed.

After the truck pulled away and the dust had settled, Henry stepped down into the road again and went on toward Franklin's. But something nagged at his mind, something unnerving, like a half-remembered nightmare. Then it came to him. The man with Pickett had hung his hand out of the truck window, and that hand had four fingers missing.

12

...

T he walk to Willie's place seemed miles longer than
it had the week before, maybe because Henry was so
anxious to talk to Willie. Since yesterday he'd been worrying about the man he'd seen in Pickett's truck. Was Pickett
in on the timber stealing? Should the deputy be told?
Willie would know what to do.

In addition to that worry, the idea that he, Henry, could
be Sarah's son haunted him day and night. Over and over
again he had told himself it wasn't possible, but sometimes it sounded like the most logical thing in the world.
He hoped Willie could tell him it wasn't true.

There was no one home, only the curious cats eyeing
him from the porch. He sat on the front step for a while,
but soon grew restless and ambled back toward the main
road. Maybe he would meet Willie coming home.

Rounding a curve, he spied Evan and Mary Beth in the
distance. They were watching something in the ditch and
did not notice Henry at first. Then Mary Beth squealed
and jumped aside and, seeing Henry, waved a hand and
smiled. Strange, them being on this lonesome road, Henry
thought, but maybe they were looking for Willie, too.

"I got a real wiggler here. Copperhead." Evan snickered as he poked a stick at the squirming snake.

"Let him go, Evan," Mary Beth urged. "He's pois'nous." Ignoring her, Evan worked the stick under the snake and lifted it aloft. Then, as it started to slide off, he tossed it into a clump of weeds. He dropped the stick and wiped his hands on the seat of his pants.

"We come to find you," he said to Henry. "Old lady Morrison wants you to come home."

"Is something wrong?" Henry asked.

"She just said to tell you the deputy is stoppin' back later and wants to talk to you. What's he want you for?"

"I don't know," Henry said. He thought of the man in Pickett's truck and looked away from Evan's questioning gaze. Maybe the deputy had caught Pickett and the other men stealing more timber.

The three of them walked abreast in the dirt road, Evan kicking a stone in front of him, Mary Beth humming to herself. Evan stopped so suddenly that Henry thought he must have seen another snake.

"Say, I know a shortcut through the woods to the Morrison place. Let's cut up over here," he said, already starting up the bank.

"Well . . ." Henry hesitated. "Are you sure it's shorter? I need to get back as soon as I can."

"Sure, it's a lot shorter — just a few ups and downs, that's all. I been this way lots of times. Come on."

Evan waded through the weeds and up the bank, Henry

and Mary Beth trailing behind. They entered a level field that had been farmed years earlier but now was overgrown with weeds and young trees. By the time they had struggled through to the far woods, they were sweating and thirsty.

"Come on. There's a run at the bottom of the hill," Evan said.

They started out walking but soon gained momentum on the steep slope. Jumping over clumps of weeds, fighting to stay upright, they stumbled the last few yards downhill and collapsed beside the stream. It took them a minute or so to catch their breath. Then Henry and Evan splashed water on their arms and faces, while Mary Beth dropped on her hands and knees and began to build a fragile dam with gravel from the stream bottom.

They followed the stream for a short distance, then worked their way up the hill on the other side. Evan's powerful legs carried him well ahead of Henry and Mary Beth. They were more than ready for a rest when Evan stopped and climbed astraddle a dead log bleached and smoothed by years of weather. One sturdy branch pointed skyward like a long-barreled cannon.

"I'll shoot down some Japs," Evan said, sighting along the limb and making a chattering noise in his throat.

"Lemme try it," Mary Beth whined.

"Naw, girls don't fight wars . . . only men."

"I don't like war. It killed Lyle Franklin," she said. Her glance met Henry's, then slid away.

116·

"He just got in the way of a bullet," Evan said. "You gotta be careful in a war and git them before they git you." Henry wondered how Evan knew so much about war.

Several tall trees shaded the crest of the hill. Hanging from one, just within reach, was a grapevine, rattling in the light wind. Mary Beth grabbed it and swung out, dropping a few feet downhill. The boys took a turn on it too before heading on down the slope.

Evan trotted into the lead, but when a briar snagged his shirt, he stopped and motioned Henry on. A little way farther down, Henry paused to survey the hollow below, choked with underbrush. He was beginning to wish he'd stayed on the road. Even after they got through the hollow, they'd still have another hill to climb.

Suddenly Henry heard an odd noise and, glancing back up the slope, saw Mary Beth frozen in midstride, eyes fastened on the nearby weeds. Evan had disappeared.

"What happened?" Henry shouted.

"He just dropped down in the ground!" the girl said.

"What!" Henry scrambled back up the hill and stared at the gaping hole as big around as a washtub. He edged toward it, then lay down and crawled the last few feet, peering over the rim. It was some kind of shaft. Its timbered walls, what he could see of them, were rotten and crumbling. One piece of freshly broken wood marked the spot of Evan's fall. Evan was down in that awful darkness. Hurt — or worse!

Henry swallowed once, then again, and called out in a wavering voice, "Evan . . ." He listened, pushing himself forward a little, leaning into the shaft. He felt Mary Beth beside him and saw her small fingers clawing at the edge of the hole.

"Not too close. The sides might cave in," he warned. Then once more he called, "Evan . . ."

"Did you hear that?" He turned to Mary Beth. He could not be sure he'd heard anything, he wanted an answer so badly.

"I think so." Her eyes filled with tears.

Henry slid forward until his chest rested on the shaft's loose rim. He cupped his hand above his eyes to shut out the sun and peered into a blackness that was blacker than any night he'd ever seen. From out of the hole came a faint moan.

"Evan . . . are you hurt?"

They both strained to hear the answer and finally it came, one muffled, paralyzing word. "Yeah."

Mary Beth's face puckered. "How we gonna git him out?" she asked.

Henry's mind raced with possibilities. While he puzzled what to do, he caught a dull glimmer of light below, a shadowy reflection that made his stomach hurt. Water! Evan might drown before they could do anything.

Henry knew they must get help, but he had to find out if there really was water down there. "Evan, can you hear me?" His voice reverberated against the walls, then seemed to be swallowed up in the inky depths.

"Yeah," came the hoarse reply.

"Is there water down there?"

"A little." Henry and Mary Beth exchanged a hopeful glance.

From the sound of Evan's voice, Henry guessed that the floor of the shaft lay just beyond the lighted section of wall. He remembered the grapevine at the top of the hill and wondered if it would be long enough to reach the bottom.

"Evan, if we drop a vine down, can you climb up?"

It was quiet for so long that Henry was afraid Evan had died. "I can't move my legs," came the weak voice at last.

Henry leaned back on his heels and looked at the blue sky. The sun was well to the west, but they still had a couple of hours before full dark. He turned to Mary Beth. She too had scooted back to a sitting position and now studied his face, waiting, her slender body trembling. It wouldn't do to leave her here while he went for help, but he couldn't leave Evan alone, either.

"You'll have to go get someone," he said to her and she sprang to her feet at once.

He jumped up to delay her for a moment. "Go to Sarah. We need a man — men — and rope. Tell her — tell her to hurry."

Mary Beth's solemn eyes held his a moment, then she turned to go.

"Wait!" Henry said. Laying a hand on her shoulder, he walked a few steps down the hill with her, pointing into the hollow. "Go down through there and up the other side. Keep the sun on your left. The road should be just on the other side of that hill." She frowned. With greater confidence then he felt, he squeezed her shoulder. "You'll find it . . . just over that hill."

She glanced back at the hole, her lips drawn thin and tight. "Is he gonna be all right?" she asked in a high, shaky voice.

Taking a deep breath to steady his own voice, Henry said, "We'll get him out."

Mary Beth stared at him, then unexpectedly, sweetly, she smiled. "Yeah," she breathed, then took off running at breakneck speed down the steep slope.

Henry watched until she reached the bottom. In the fringe of brush she paused and looked up. At that distance Henry could not make out her features, only the still, poised urgency in her figure as she raised a hand and waved. Henry blinked back a rush of tears, and when he could see again, she was gone. Slowly he walked back uphill, crawled to the edge of the shaft, and stared down.

A dank, earthy smell rose out of the hole, the odor of a place that had been undisturbed for years. Henry guessed that the hole was an abandoned mine shaft, covered over long ago but not filled. He heard a faint sound, as though something had plopped into water.

"Evan," he called. There was only a grunt in reply. "I sent Mary Beth for help. They'll be here pretty soon." Oh, how he hoped that was true!

As he lay there, Henry thought of the day he'd first met Evan and immediately disliked him, then of the day they had fought and Henry had ached to beat the tar out of him. Somehow, that had been the turning point. The day of the haying Evan had given him the knife, trying, clumsily, to be friends, and Henry had begun to believe that maybe they could get along after all. Now Evan lay at the bottom of this shaft, hurt, maybe dying. Henry tried to push the frightful thought out of his mind.

Every few minutes he called down to let Evan know he was still there, while the sun moved steadily westward and pushed long ragged shadows out across the hillside. Time was getting short. He tried to think of what he would do if help didn't come by dark.

When the sun sank behind the trees and a gray haze crept up out of the hollow, Henry knew he couldn't sit there any longer and do nothing. He leaned over the edge and studied the dim walls. If he pressed his back to one wall of the shaft and wedged his feet against the opposite wall, he thought, he ought to be able to work his way down. As he swung his legs over the edge, loose globs of dirt fell away in a fading whisper. Trying to shut out the mental image of the black pit beneath him, he crept downward, concentrating on the single task of finding a place for each foot.

He heard his shirt rip, then one foot slipped off a wet timber, and he pushed hard against the sides to keep from falling. "You can do it," he muttered through clenched teeth, arms and legs straining to hold against the downward pull. In that stiff, uneasy crouch, he looked up at the jagged square of sky and the high cirrus clouds still bright with sun. Then he turned back to the job he had set for himself.

The damp blackness rose to meet him and the walls grew ever dimmer. When the light no longer reached him, he had to feel the wall to find each foothold. Progress now was in slow, deliberate inches. At last he felt water, and gingerly he lowered himself to the flooded floor of the shaft. At that very moment he realized that he was marooned down there as surely as Evan was, because neither of them could climb back up without help. He held his breath and listened.

Hearing nothing, he spoke aloud. "Evan, where are you?"

"Here," came the gruff voice, very near.

Waving his arms like insect antennae, Henry finally found Evan's hand. It was cold and jerked at his touch. He groped along Evan's arm, the back of his hand, his rising and falling shoulders. "Are you hurt bad?"

"My legs . . . they feel like fire."

Henry strained to see. It was strange, knowing his eyes were wide open, but seeing nothing. In his mind he pictured how the pit must look, moist timbered walls, pools of black water, rocky crevices hiding ugly, slithering creatures. He rubbed his eyes with the backs of his hands, then fumbled in the darkness for Evan. The big boy lay on his stomach, pinned beneath a rocky mound of earth with only his head and shoulders exposed.

"Evan, I've got to get this dirt off of you."

"Don't touch my legs," Evan pleaded.

"If I uncover your legs, you can sit up," Henry argued, knowing that sooner or later Evan would have to be dug out.

He began pulling away handfuls of the wet earth. Once, when he lifted a slimy timber, Evan groaned deep in his throat and shifted his body, sending soft ripples against Henry's bare feet. Finally, Henry uncovered a wet pantleg. He brushed off the dirt, then felt along the leg.

"Is this where it's hurt?" Henry asked, running his fingers over the ankle already tight and hot.

"Yeah. Is it broken?"

"I don't know, but it's swelled pretty big."

"How about my other leg? It hurts terrible."

"I don't have all the dirt off yet," Henry said. He leaned forward and began pulling away more dirt, lifting out rocks and chunks of wood and dropping them behind him. Parts of the shaft's wooden walls must have been knocked loose by Evan's fall. Henry tried not to think of that awful plunge into darkness. He came across a thick piece of timber, and when he moved it slightly, Evan screamed.

The sound rocked Henry back on his heels. "Aw, I'm sorry," he said.

There was no reply for a moment, then Evan spoke. "Go ahead and dig. I won't yell no more." Henry moved one small handful of dirt at a time until at last the timber lay exposed.

"I'm going to lift it off now," Henry said.

"Yeah, go ahead."

Henry rose to his feet and leaned across to get a good grip on the timber, then lifted it straight up and dropped it behind him. As it came away, Evan uttered a croaking sound and then was still.

"That ought to feel better." When Evan didn't respond, Henry spoke his name, "Evan. Evan." Then he whispered to himself, "Don't die . . . please don't die."

Laying a hand on Evan's back, Henry felt his slow, rhythmic breathing. At least he was still alive. Henry continued brushing away the dirt, then inch by inch examined the leg. A long gash just below the knee was wet and sticky. No wonder Evan had screamed.

Henry looked straight up at the small square of gray light above and wondered if Mary Beth had reached the Morrison place yet. For a moment Sarah's face rose before him. He could imagine her fright when Mary Beth blurted out the story, and her frantic haste to get help. She would feel responsible because she had sent Evan to find him.

Suddenly Evan groaned. Henry laid a hand on his shoulder. "It's all right. Just don't move."

"What happened?"

"I guess you passed out."

"Hell, I never done that before," Evan breathed.

"Can you move your left leg?" Henry asked. The movement sent water lapping against Henry with the softness of cool velvet. "You've got a bad cut on your other leg."

"I wanna turn on my back and git my face outa this water."

"Do you think you can?"

"I'll do it," came Evan's reply, his voice weak but with a hint of the old belligerence.

Afraid to help, Henry sat and listened to the struggle, the grunts of pain, the splashes that reminded him of a bass wallowing in the shallows. Then with one final wrenching moan, Evan lay still. "How'd you git down here?" he asked.

"Climbed down," Henry said.

"What for?"

"I figured you could use some company."

"Yeah," Evan said. Several moments passed before he spoke again. "I think I see a star. Is it dark already?"

Henry stiffened. Where was Mary Beth? She'd surely had time to get help and return. The directions he'd given her were simple, just go up over the hill and down to the road. But he wasn't sure of them; he'd simply told her what Evan had told him. He hoped Evan had been right about the road. Once Mary Beth found it, she'd know the way.

"I guess it don't really matter," Henry said. "We're already in the dark."

"You think the water's gettin' deeper?" Evan asked.

"Can't tell," Henry said, "but maybe there's some dry ground around here." He stood up and groped for the wall behind him, then slowly followed it around to his left, feeling his way past Evan. The shaft walls were uneven, the timbers pushed outward by the pressing earth. Every step was deliberate, exploratory, because he was afraid of stepping on Evan or, worse yet, falling in another hole.

"What'd you find?" Evan called.

"Nothing here but wet walls and wet floor. You think this was part of a coal mine?"

"Probably an air shaft. The Walthrop mine ran through here."

Henry straightened up and cracked his head on a protruding rock. Upon closer examination, he realized it was the roof of a horizontal passageway. Inching ahead, he stretched out his arms and felt both sides of the shaft. He moved forward, sliding his hands along the walls, raking the floor with his bare feet. If this was an intersecting shaft, it must lead somewhere, maybe to the surface.

His feet made no sound as step by cautious step he advanced along the corridor. When he felt the tunnel slope downward, he stopped. He sure didn't want to go deeper. The return trip proved less difficult for now he knew, if only by touch, that the passageway was clear of hazards. When he thought he was nearing the vertical shaft, he called Evan's name.

"Yeah, where you been? I thought maybe you fell in a hole, too."

"Nope. I found a shaft leading off this one." Henry

looked up, but there was no surface light now, just a patch of black sky spangled with stars.

"It don't make no difference. I can't go nowhere," Evan mumbled.

"They'll be here pretty soon anyway," Henry replied, but he was beginning to wonder about Mary Beth. She must have reached the farm by this time. Unless something had happened to her.

Henry tried to dismiss that thought. She just had to bring help because nobody else knew where they were or what had happened to them. But he could not keep from worrying that she might be hurt or lost, unable to deliver the life-and-death message she carried.

13

###

"You know, I'm getting used to the dark," Henry said in what he hoped was a casual voice. "Maybe I'm getting eyes in my fingers. There's an old woman in Gorleyville who's been blind all her life. She's seventy-seven now. She says she has eyes in her fingers."

"Well, maybe it's better we can't see," Evan said. "No tellin' what's crawlin' around down here."

"You weren't scared of that copperhead on the road," Henry reminded him.

"Naw, but I could see him." Evan groaned and churned the still water. "My legs must be broke. I ain't never hurt this bad in my whole life."

"What about when that horse kicked you?" Henry queried, hoping to take Evan's mind off of his legs.

"I wasn't kicked by no horse. At least, not lately."

"You said over at the store that a horse kicked you."

"Oh, that. Naw, that was my dad."

"He hit you?" Henry asked.

"Yeah, when he gits mad, he hits anybody close."

Henry pulled his knees to his chest, circled his arms

around them, and rested his forehead against his wet trousers. Mr. Compton had never raised his voice in anger to any member of the Compton family. When Mrs. Compton threatened the boys with a whipping, he would chide her about her temper and say they were just acting like boys.

"You know, once in a while Dad does something nice," Evan said, "but when he gits mad, he's . . . he's real mean."

"I guess being mean is kind of like being sick, only you can't take medicine for it," Henry said.

"If only they'd take me in the army," Evan said. "Soon as I'm old enough, I'm leaving this place."

"It isn't so bad here," Henry countered, then grinned and added, "I'm talking about the valley, not this hole in the ground."

"How you reckon they'll get us outa here?" Evan asked. It was a question Henry had asked himself quite a few times since he'd descended into the shaft. Maybe with a rope tied around their waists, and with some strong men pulling from above, they could make it up the slippery walls. Henry thought he could, but he wasn't sure Evan could do it, especially if one of his legs was broken.

"Henry, there ain't nobody comin' tonight," Evan said at last. "Sis won't be able to find this place again, not in the dark."

"If they don't come tonight, they'll be here tomorrow." Henry spoke the reassuring words he would've liked to hear someone speak to him. "Mary Beth will show 'em where to look."

"Reckon we have to sleep down in this hellhole then," Evan muttered.

They grew quiet and for the first time heard rumbling thunder above. Henry peered up the shaft, but the star-filled sky had disappeared. A flash of lightening illuminated the opening for a fraction of a second, then all was black again.

"Looks like a storm up there," Henry said.

"Say, ain't we lucky we're in outa the rain," Evan said.

"Yep. I'd sure hate to get wet," Henry said, laughing. Then in a soft voice Evan began to sing. "Though April showers may come your way . . ." He stopped and laughed, a low, breathless laugh that didn't quite hide his pain.

"Go ahead, finish it," Henry urged.

There was no uneasiness between them as Evan sang. When he stopped, Henry said, "You sure have a good voice."

"You oughta hear Mom; she can really sing. But she don't sing much anymore." He paused a moment, then continued. "I reckon it's 'cause of Dad."

"What do you mean?" Henry asked, but knew very well what misery Earl Pickett might inflict on those around him.

"Well, she's sick a lot. I don't mind him hittin' me, but when he hits Mom, I just . . . I wish he was dead." Henry caught his breath.

"I try to do what he says, but sometimes I just can't."

After a long pause, Evan went on. "Did you ever drown a cat?"

The chilling question made Henry stiffen. "Nope," he said, feeling his lips curl.

"Well, he give me a burlap sack of kittens awhile back and told me to take 'em down to the crick and drown 'em. I took 'em but I couldn't do it. I gave 'em to the McCrary sisters. They love cats."

"Why did he want you to drown 'em?"

"'Cause we had so many," Evan said. "He said he had too many kids and too many cats, but at least he could git rid of the cats."

They sat awhile in silence. Many times in the last months Henry had mourned the loss of his father, but now he began to understand that there were worse things than not having a father. He stretched out his legs and listened to the growling thunder above ground. Lightning flashed continually. Soon the dull sizzle of rain reached his ears, and a wayward drop struck his upturned face. This could be a real gully-washer, he thought.

Evan took no notice of the threatening weather. His thoughts were still on his father. "I know there ain't many people who like him. I don't much myself. And the men he brings around . . . I don't like them neither."

Henry remembered the man in the truck with Pickett. "Do you know a man who has the fingers missing on his right hand?" he asked.

"Sure, that's Bailey Moore. He lost his fingers in a mowing machine. Where'd you meet him?"

"I saw him in your dad's truck the other day."

"Yeah, he comes to the house sometimes . . . on business."

"They steal trees, don't they?" Henry asked in a flat voice.

"How'd you know?"

"I came across Moore and another fellow in the woods, loading up some trees. I found out later the trees belonged to Sarah."

"Yeah, well, they're stealin' 'em all right," Evan said.

"The deputy's going to catch those men one of these days," Henry said. "That's probably why he wanted to see me. I know what they look like."

"Did the other fella have a scar across his eyebrow?" Evan inquired, and when Henry said he did, Evan expelled his breath noisily. "He comes to see Dad, too. I reckon they're all in it together."

Henry wanted to console Evan, but what could he say? That his father was sure to go to prison?

"You like your dad?" Evan asked.

"Yep . . . but he died in February."

"I didn't know that," Evan said.

"He wasn't my real dad. He just took me in to live with them."

"Then where's your real mom and dad?"

"I don't know."

Suddenly there was a creaking noise from up in the shaft, then an avalanche of water and wet earth came pouring down on them. In an instant Henry had squeezed back against the wall with his arms up to protect his head. He could hear Evan grunting as he tried to pull himself out of the torrent. When a falling timber grazed Henry's arm, he knew they had to get out of there. He bolted across the shaft and stumbled against Evan.

"We've got to go back in the passageway," he shouted and wrenched Evan to his feet. "Hang on to me." With his arm encircling Evan's waist, they lurched along the wall. This time when Henry cracked his head on the overhang, he felt only relief. That solid rock was their salvation. As soon as they ducked under it, they were free of the deluge, though they could hear its dull roar behind them.

"What happened?" Evan gasped, and sagged to his knees.

"No, we can't stay here." Henry strained to pull the big boy up, goaded by the gentle stream creeping over his toes. "Come on. We've got to get in farther." In his mind, he could picture the floor of the shaft inundated, with mud already spilling along the passageway.

They moved slower now, Evan limping, cursing the pain, Henry trying to support him and yet keep one hand out in front. The noise of the cave-in gradually died away. Finally Evan dropped to the floor, moaning. Henry was glad to be free of the load and he sank down, too. When he thought about what had happened, he began to shiver. He clamped his teeth tightly to keep them from chattering.

Escape up the vertical shaft was impossible now. When the rescuers came, they would find only the remnant of a shaft buried under muddy debris. He and Evan were on their own, trapped in this labyrinth of deteriorating mine passages. It was possible that one might lead to the surface, but maybe all of them were sealed forever. Henry admitted the stark truth, but only to himself. No one could help them now.

"Are you all right?" He groped until he felt Evan's shoulder.

"I been better," Evan mumbled. Henry began to scratch at the wet mud caked in his hair and on his arms and shoulders. In the stillness he could hear Evan doing the same thing.

"You suppose this is how the movie stars feel when they git a mudpack?" Evan began laughing, but it was a hollow laugh with quick gasps of breath that soon changed to broken sobs. Whether Evan's fear was contagious or Henry simply gave in to his own fears didn't really matter. Tears came, and raising his hands to his face, Henry wept too.

Many minutes passed before either spoke again. Finally Evan said, "I didn't mean to be a crybaby. . . . but we ain't never gonna git outa here, are we?"

"I don't know," Henry replied honestly, wiping his face on his arm. "But I'm not giving up yet. We'll just rest awhile, then get started. If we follow this tunnel, maybe we'll find an opening."

"What if there ain't no opening? And if there is, how are we gonna find it in the dark?"

"We just keep going," Henry said, his voice echoing along the shaft. "And the sooner we find our way out, the sooner we get something to eat. I'm starved."

"Me too." Evan's voice sounded weak and hopeless. "But I don't think I kin walk."

"You have to walk," Henry stated flatly. "Whether it hurts or not. Here, I'll help you." He dragged Evan up and pulled the boy's arm around his shoulders, walking a little in front so he could run one hand along the wall. Evan groaned at every step.

As they proceeded, Henry sniffed the air. The passage must have been closed up for years because the air was stale and dank. He wondered if they would eventually reach a place where there was no air at all.

Doggedly he kept on, holding Evan up, keeping him going with the words, "Just a little farther." They walked on for what seemed like hours until Evan slumped to the floor.

Henry scouted ahead, trying to memorize the feel of the shaft. The corridor sloped downward for a way, then leveled off. Moving ahead, Henry stumbled and fell forward on his hands and knees. He had tripped over a narrow iron track. He ran his hand along it to his right but it ended abruptly against a wall. Following it back the other way, he stood up, turning his head one direction, then the other, sensing an openness and a noticeable difference in the air. He must have come into a room.

He inched his bare foot along the track, stooping to dig away the dirt when he lost contact with the metal. He followed it several more feet, then stopped. He should not get too far from Evan. He turned back along the track until he reached the wall. Once again in the corridor, he located Evan by the sounds of his heavy breathing.

"Are you ready to go on?" he asked.

"Do we have to?" Evan's voice rattled.

"We've got to get ourselves out," Henry said, saying aloud what he'd been silently repeating over and over to himself since the cave-in. "But I reckon we can rest awhile," he added, dropping down beside Evan.

"I feel like I been awake for days," Evan said.

"Yeah, me too," Henry replied. He leaned back against the cold earth wall and closed his eyes. In some strange way it felt good to be able to sit there and not have to make any decisions. The blackness was a cocoon around him that let his body relax until he could feel the dull thumping of his heart. After a while he heard Evan's slow, regular breaths and knew that the injured boy had gone to sleep.

While his body rested, Henry's mind searched for plans of escape. There was really only one thing to do: They must follow the iron track and trust that it would lead them to the surface. At least it was better than sitting there in the darkness and letting their hope die away.

A few minutes later, when he heard Evan stirring, Henry reached out and touched his shoulder.

"Huh . . . What . . . is that you, Henry?"

"Yeah, we'd better be moving," Henry said.

They struggled to their feet and trod slowly along the corridor. When they started down the gentle slope, Evan complained. "We ain't goin' deeper, are we?"

"Just a little bit, then it levels off. I found some track. We'll follow it. Maybe it goes . . . somewhere."

Henry moved through the black room, practically dragging Evan, while he tried to keep one foot on the rail. When Evan begged to stop, Henry left him and felt ahead, sensing at once when the walls closed in on him again and he entered another passageway. A terrible lump rose in his throat. Were they going to wander around in this blackness until finally they would just have to give up and lie down and die? He sat down and rubbed his gritty eyes. He'd better quit thinking like that and keep moving. It was the only way they would ever get out.

He crept back to Evan. "The track goes into another shaft," he said. "Whenever you're ready, we'll go on."

"I wish I had something to wrap around my ankle. It don't wanna hold me up."

"I could use my shirt," Henry volunteered, remembering he'd torn it climbing down the shaft. He slipped it off, took out the knife Evan had given him, and cut off several pieces. Working together, they bound the swollen ankle and tied a tight knot with the last strip.

"That feels better already," Evan said as he got to his feet.

They set off again, following the track into one room

after another, losing all sense of time and distance. Their rests were frequent, their steps heavy, with Evan leaning more and more on Henry. The blackness had become commonplace so that sometimes Henry thought he was actually seeing the things he was touching. They walked, then rested, then walked again. As the hours passed, despair rose in Henry until it almost choked him.

They knew they had entered another room when their voices echoed from the high ceiling. The cold steel track led them on, into a corridor that narrowed until their shoulders brushed the walls.

Evan snapped to a sudden stop. "What was that?" he gasped.

"What? I don't hear anything."

"I felt something touch my ear. Gawd! What was it?" Evan's voice rose. "Listen!"

From up in front of them came a faint sound, like marbles rattling together. Step by hesitant step they moved forward, drawing nearer to the sound, though it was hard to pinpoint its location. All around them there seemed to be a circulation of whisperings and flutterings. Then Henry felt something flit by him, not touching him but fanning him with its passing flight.

"Bats!" Evan's hopeful voice exploded into the darkness like a flash of lightning.

"What? Here?" Henry ducked and threw his hands over his head, hunching his shoulders to ward off an attack.

"Yeah, bats! Don't you see . . . they're in here, but they have a way out. All we gotta do is find it." In his excitement Evan let go of Henry, his legs buckled under him, and he fell groaning and laughing at Henry's feet. "If they're inside now, it must be daylight. Do you see any light?"

Henry circled slowly in the unbroken darkness. "Nope. You stay here. I'll look around." He edged forward, hearing the whistling movements overhead as well as his own chattering teeth. But, he resolved, whatever he had to do to get out he would do, even if it meant beating off a whole horde of bats.

All was black, a cold familiar blackness. Then in the space of one step he saw it, a dim gray flush of light high up on his left. It was a mere slit at first, but as he moved forward and the ground rose beneath him, he caught a glimpse of blue sky.

"Yahoo!" he whooped. "I found it! Evan, I found it!" Then his legs gave way and he sank down in a heap. Tears filled his eyes and seemed to wash away the darkness, for now he could see his mud-spattered trousers, his grimy hands, the dim walls rising to that glorious patch of light.

He closed his eyes just for the sheer joy of opening them again and seeing light. Then he rose to his feet and scrambled up a ramp of loose dirt until he could see weeds just outside the hole swaying gently in the wind, and above them, a clear bright sky.

Slowly he reached up and touched a shining blade of

grass. Then he slid back down the slope on the seat of his pants, calling out as he went, "It's easy, Evan. We'll be out in no time."

While they hobbled through the semi-darkness, the twittering sounds of the bats settling down to rest came from the dark recesses of the cavern. Just short of the surface, Henry paused. "I'll climb out, then haul you up," he suggested, and when Evan nodded, he pulled himself through the opening, breathing in the fresh air. The sunlight blinded him and he squeezed his eyes shut until he peered through thin slits. They had been in the mine almost a whole day, because the sun was already well to the west.

"Take my hands," Henry said. He pulled and Evan climbed and soon they lay side by side in the grass. When they sat up and got a good look at each other, they burst out laughing. They were covered with mud from their heads to their bare feet. It had dried on their skin in lumps and in smooth, gilded layers that cracked with every movement.

Once the giddiness had passed, they looked around them, down the steep, weedy hillside to Wynnton sprawling along the railroad track. "Gawd, I never thought we'd make it," Evan said.

"We were lucky," Henry said. "We could have been in there forever."

"Henry, if it hadn't been for you . . ." Evan stopped and spread his hands.

"You'd have done the same thing for me," Henry said.

14
...

Henry pointed to Evan's leg and the dirty, blood-caked wound. "Guess you need to see a doctor," he said.

Evan gestured toward Wynnton. "It ain't far to Doc Hurst's place. He can fix me up."

They worked their way down the slope, Henry in front, Evan leaning on his shoulder, until they finally reached the bank above the gravel road. With slow, careful steps Henry helped Evan down into the roadway. Walking there was wonderfully easy compared with walking in total darkness, but Henry knew Evan was still hurting.

"You think they're up there at the shaft looking for us?" Henry asked.

"I reckon. Mom's probably worried sick. This is all my fault. If I'd been watchin' where I was goin'. . . ."

"It was just an accident," Henry said. "Any of us could have fallen in that hole. But I know one thing," he added, grinning. "Next time you want to take a shortcut, I'm not going."

"Hell, next time I ain't neither."

When they finally crossed the covered bridge and came to the edge of town, a woman ducked under her clothesline and hurried out to the front gate.

"Evan Pickett! It's you! You're safe. We thought you were . . ." She stopped herself, then looked at Henry. "And you're Sarah Morrison's boy." It was an innocent remark that Henry accepted with a lopsided grin. They continued toward the house Evan pointed out, a neat, white home with a picket fence around it and a sign in the yard identifying it as the doctor's residence.

Mrs. Hurst admitted them to the office and called to her husband. A thin, gray-haired man entered the room, his eyes lighting with recognition. Henry wondered if everyone in town knew about them.

"Well, boys, you made it out," he said, sizing them up — the dried mud, Evan's wrapped ankle, the torn pantleg stained with blood. He wasted no time. "Evan, I'll want you in the next room. How about you, Henry? Are you hurt?"

"Nope, just awful dirty."

The doctor turned to his wife. "Edna, ring up Carrie Peterson and have her send young Lem up to the Morrison place to let them know the boys are all right."

While the doctor helped Evan into the adjoining room, Mrs. Hurst vanished into another part of the house. She returned shortly with a pan of water and a bright yellow washcloth and towel.

"You can wash up in here while I help the doctor," she

said, giving Henry's shoulder a motherly pat. Henry did the best he could, but the water soon turned to a thick brown gravy. Faintly he could hear voices rumbling in the next room, the doctor's deep and matter-of-fact, Edna's soothing, and once a yelp from Evan.

When he had finished washing, Henry sat down in a chair and dropped his head into his hands. He felt so tired! Missing one whole night's sleep was bad enough, but it was nothing compared with the drain of those long, hopeless hours underground. It was like a half-forgotten dream. And even now, away from the mine passages, their dank smell seemed to hang in the air.

Henry was beginning to doze off when Evan hobbled through the door on a pair of crutches. The mud was gone from his face and arms, and both legs were bandaged. He looked like the old Evan, but Henry would never again see him as a bully or an enemy.

"How are the legs now?" Henry asked.

"Almost good as new, thanks to the doc," Evan said. Taking a few awkward steps across the room, he managed to walk on the crutches without stumbling.

"I'll run you boys up to the Morrison place," Doc Hurst said. "Everyone's up there."

During the short ride, the doctor reached over and patted Henry's shoulder. "Evan told me what happened. You sure did something, Henry, starting on the back side of that ridge and working your way clear through to the other end. It must have been more than a mile." Henry had not thought about distance down there, only about time, the black time that might stretch on to eternity.

When they arrived, Henry recognized Mrs. Franklin on the porch. He didn't know the other woman on the swing or the boy about Evan's age lounging in the grass.

Mrs. Franklin rushed down the steps to meet them. "Thank God you boys are safe!" She hugged them and pulled them toward the porch. "Are you hurt bad?" she asked Evan.

"I got a cut and a sprained ankle, but Doc bandaged 'em."

Mrs. Franklin and the woman she called Helen soon had them at the kitchen table with plates of steaming food before them, and they hovered nearby while the boys ate. Where was Sarah? Henry wondered. It seemed strange, with her absent and the two women so confidently occupying her kitchen. But, Henry concluded, these women probably would be at home in anybody's kitchen. He had never tasted food so good.

When she saw they had finished, Mrs. Franklin dropped into a chair across from Henry. "Wayne was here when Lem brought the news. He went up to get the others. They've been up there digging all night and all day."

"Where's Mary Beth?" Evan asked.

"She's up there. They couldn't get her to leave. Your mother is up there too," she told him. "And Sarah," she added, glancing at Henry.

Henry had been wondering about Mary Beth, too.

They hadn't mentioned her since they waited at the bottom of the shaft for her to bring help, but Evan must have been thinking of her all along.

Moments later they heard an uproar outside. Car doors slammed, then there were quick steps in the gravel, and the mounting clamor of many voices. Suddenly a thin, wild-eyed woman plunged through the door. She hesitated only a moment, then swept over to take Evan in her arms. Her sobs were lost in the noisy commotion of the kitchen, the men's voices rumbling like thunder, the women's high-pitched.

Henry was separated from Evan and quickly surrounded by people, some he knew, some strangers, but all smiling and happy. Wayne clasped his hand and said, "A good job, partner."

"You're mighty brave, son," Mr. Franklin added. Willie's welcome face stood out in the crowd. Just then Henry saw Sarah. She came through the door and stopped in midstride, her eyes blazing as she saw Henry across the room. The anguish of the long night was plain on her face.

Sarah started toward him, and for an instant Henry thought she was going to run and hug him as Mrs. Pickett had hugged Evan. But something stopped her. A moment later she knelt beside Evan with a hand on his knee, peering into his weary face. She probably felt the accident was her fault, Henry thought, because she had sent Evan on the errand to find him. As she spoke to the big boy, Henry saw Evan nod his head and smile. How he envied

Evan that concern, that gentle touch, that look of joyful relief!

It was strange how everyone grew quiet just then, so that even in the farthest corner they heard when Sarah asked Evan, "What happened?"

Finding himself the center of attention, Evan seemed to rise in his chair, to take on size and importance.

"Well, I was just walkin' along and all of a sudden I was in the dark. I figured I'd fell in an old mine shaft. I been in mines before so I wasn't scared." He stopped and looked over at Henry. Their eyes held for several moments, then they both grinned.

Evan took a deep breath, lifted his chin, and began again. "If it wasn't for Henry, I'd still be down there." All eyes turned toward Henry. He wished he could crawl under the table. Instead he pushed his hands deep in his pockets and stared at his dirty feet.

"Tell us, Evan," someone prompted.

Beginning with the frightening fall, which he said he could barely remember, Evan went on to that moment when he realized that Henry was there beside him at the bottom of the shaft. When he recounted the horror of the mudslide, the room filled with hushed whisperings, and when he told of the bats, the listeners murmured their satisfaction. After the story was finished, everyone seemed to talk at once; then, assured that the all-night ordeal was happily concluded, they began to leave.

It was then that Henry noticed Mary Beth peering

through the screen door. He went over, but before he could speak, she blurted out, "I got lost . . . I jes' . . . got lost."

Henry pushed open the door and drew her inside. "It doesn't matter. You did your job. Anyway, we got out," Henry said, patting her thin shoulders. "Evan's all right. Come and see."

"Hey, Sis, I been lookin' for you," Evan said. "Where you been?"

"Out on the porch," she mumbled. Her steps lagged and Henry could see she dreaded facing her brother's questions.

Evan got straight to the point. "What happened when you went for help?" he asked bluntly.

"I got lost," she repeated. "It was almost dark 'fore I found the road. Then after we got help, I couldn't find the hole again." Relieved when she'd told her side of the story, she began to quiz the boys about the night in the mine.

"I tell you, Sis, when I figured out them was bats flyin' around us, I knew we was gonna git out," Evan said. "That was better than Christmas."

Tires scattering gravel signaled someone else's arrival, and glancing out the door, Henry saw Earl Pickett stomping toward the porch, his big hands balled into fists.

"Come in, Mr. Pickett," Sarah called as he came up on the porch.

"I come for my family. I guess they caused everybody

enough trouble." As soon as he stepped inside, his eyes fastened on Evan. The boy grabbed his crutches and started to stand up, but his father's words stopped him.

"Why the hell don't you watch where you're goin'? It takes a real jackass to fall in a hole in the ground. I oughta whip you good," he added, stepping forward as if he would do just what he threatened, then and there.

For a moment everyone in the room seemed paralyzed, then Henry stepped over in front of Evan. But before he could say anything to Pickett, a firm hand pulled him aside.

"It was an accident, Mr. Pickett," Sarah said. "Thank goodness the boys weren't badly hurt."

Pickett folded his arms across his chest and glared at her. Then, red-faced, he turned to his wife. "Git up outa there. We're goin' home."

With that, he spun on his heels and slammed out the screen door. Mrs. Pickett hurried Mary Beth and Evan toward the door, casting a quick, grateful glance in Henry's direction.

On the porch, Evan paused and lifted a hand to Henry, more a salute than a wave. Henry grinned and returned the gesture. No words were needed. Those hours in the mine were something special between them, something scary, but something good, too. And he knew that sometime they would talk about that night, even laugh about it.

Once everyone was gone, Henry slumped into the porch swing. A numbness seemed to envelop him and drain away his energy, and he wondered how he would ever get up the stairs to bed.

Sarah appeared at the door. "Thank goodness this day is over," she said.

"Were you up there all night?" Henry asked.

"Yes. We had trouble finding the shaft in the dark. Then, when we saw the hole filled with mud, we thought . . . we just knew . . ." She did not finish.

"I'm sorry we caused so much trouble."

"What I can't understand is why you went down in that shaft." Her voice was flat, controlled, almost polite. "Why did you?"

"I don't know," Henry said. "After I got down there, I asked myself the same question."

"We could have found you quicker if you had just stayed near the shaft. We might have got there before it caved in. You know, you could have died in there."

"I thought a lot about that while we were wandering around down below," Henry said, grinning.

Sarah pushed open the door and stepped out to face him. "There was nothing funny about it, and I'm sure the people who were up there all night digging didn't think it was amusing." The anger faded as she continued. "Don't you know I could — we could — have lost you. How could I live . . ."

She did not complete the sentence, but instead turned and pulled open the screen door. A sudden loud clap made Henry jump. It was the first time he'd heard Sarah slam a door. Why was she making such a fuss over the accident? She acted as if he had done a terrible thing going down in the shaft, when all he'd wanted to do was keep Evan company.

After a long, hot bath that left him limp and dragging, Henry climbed the stairs, wondering if it would be as black in his room as it had been in the mine. He had never been afraid of the dark before. He set the lamp on the nightstand, then leaned over and blew out the cheery amber flame. Shadows seemed to come to life as he hopped into bed and pulled the quilt up to his chin. But when he saw Dandy vault up on the windowsill in search of the day's last lingering warmth, he felt himself begin to relax.

He wanted to lie there and think about the marvelous escape, he wanted to think about becoming friends with Evan. But it seemed that nothing could hold him back from the slow descent into sleep. Through his dazed mind drifted the unanswered question of what Sarah might have done if she'd thought her son was trapped underground. Then he slept.

Henry did not know what woke him, but he felt the black walls of the night around him as close and still as the mine passages he and Evan had passed through the day before. He had to get outside, out in the open air, even if it was still dark. He pulled on his clothes and felt his way down the stairs. From the porch steps he watched the first gray light bring back substance and pale color to the land. Then the sun reared over the eastern hills, brilliant and golden and wonderfully comforting.

It was not long before he heard Sarah in the kitchen. She had awakened early, too. When the tantalizing aroma of bacon became so strong that his mouth watered, he went inside. She brought plates and silverware to the table and he slid into a chair.

"You're up early," she said, then went back to the stove.

"I couldn't sleep," Henry said.

"I slept . . . a little," she said, as she carried over a skillet and lifted two eggs onto his plate. "I dreamed about you being in the mine. It's still hard for me to understand why you went down in there."

"Well, I thought I could help Evan."

Sarah stopped and stared at him with a look so penetrating that Henry had to drop his eyes to his plate.

"How were you going to help him? Didn't you think . . . didn't you realize . . ." The words rose to a shrill pitch that must have startled Sarah as much as it did Henry, because she stopped, and when she continued, her voice had returned almost to normal. "I just expected you to use better judgment."

"But he was down there by himself . . . and hurt."

"That was no reason for you to risk your life."

She took the skillet back and set it on the stove, then turned around. "I'm not used to having someone to worry about . . . I just can't . . ." She stiffened her back and took a deep breath. "Henry, I believe it would be best if you went home."

It was the last thing Henry expected to hear. He could only stare at her, disbelieving, until she turned away. Everyone had said how brave he was and what a great thing he'd done. Why should she be so angry when everyone else was so happy? He stood up to confront her.

"What about my job — the work around here?"

"I'll be able to get by until next year, then I can get someone older," she said, turning her back to him. "Having a child around . . . You don't understand. It's just . . . just too much responsibility."

She wasn't being the least bit fair. Sudden anger boiled in Henry and the words were out before he could stop them.

"Was your baby too much responsibility?"

Sarah spun around, her face ashen, eyes glittering. "How do you know about that?"

"Evan told me," Henry said. He watched her eyes turn cloudy. She looked as though she might try to defend herself, but then her features smoothed into the old familiar indifference.

"I did what I had to do," she said, turning back to the stove.

For a moment Henry was tempted to blurt out his secret thoughts. But he decided against it. Even if Sarah could believe he was her son, she still wouldn't want him.

152·

Children were too much trouble. He wished he'd never mentioned the baby. His accusing tone was meant to hurt her, and it had. The hurt was there in her stiff shoulders and in the nervous, hovering hands trying to find something to do at the stove.

He turned away, sorry that he'd deliberately tried to hurt her. She took no notice as he crossed the kitchen and went upstairs.

15
...

Once in his room, Henry pulled his suitcase out of the closet and opened it on the bed. It took only minutes to pack his clothes; then he walked to the window and gazed out over the garden. This house, this valley, felt more like home than any place he'd ever lived, and despite Sarah's rejection, he longed to stay. But he turned, picked up the suitcase and went down the hall. It wouldn't be easy walking out the back door for the last time. He called up his earlier anger to strengthen his will, but his knees still felt weak and unreliable as he stepped into the kitchen.

Sarah looked stunned when she saw the suitcase. "What are you doing?"

"I'm going home," he replied.

"But I didn't mean for you to go today. I thought you could wait and catch a ride with Doc Hurst on Saturday."

"I don't mind the walk," Henry said in a tight, restrained voice.

"But don't you want to see Willie before you go? And Evan?"

Henry noticed there was not the usual disfavor in her voice when she spoke Evan's name. Maybe she had changed her mind about him, realizing he was all right, once you got to know him. Henry had found that out, not only about Evan but about Sarah, too.

"And I was planning on you helping me pick some vegetables and take them to Wynnton on Friday." She stood there looking at him, biting her bottom lip, waiting.

Henry felt his resolve crumbling. He couldn't leave when she needed him. Besides, he wasn't looking forward to going back and having to explain why she'd sent him home.

"All right, I'll stay till then," he murmured. "Nobody is expecting me in Gorleyville anyway." He set the suitcase by the stairs, then crossed the kitchen and went out on the porch. He'd stay, but he'd keep away from her as much as he could until Saturday.

The storm had littered the yard with twigs and leaves and had blown down several large limbs from the maples. Memory of the storm was a hazy dream, thunder and lightning and rain that hardly touched him and Evan that night. Until the shaft caved in!

Henry went down and grabbed one of the thick branches and dragged it out to the brush pile by the garden. Once the larger limbs were out of the way, he began raking up the rest of the debris. He was almost finished when he saw a truck pulling into the lane. It was Pickett's truck but Willie was driving it. Henry waited under the shady maple by the porch.

"The sheriff and his deputy have arrested Pickett and

the other two men," Willie said. At that moment Sarah stepped through the door, and Willie nodded to her. "I was just telling Henry they've arrested the men who've been stealing our timber. Caught them with a load of real nice oaks, and on my land too."

"Well, that's good news," Sarah said, though Henry heard no satisfaction in her voice.

"Pickett was one of them," Willie added.

"Pickett!" Sarah said. "I can't believe he would . . . yes, I guess I can believe it."

"They confessed they have some of the logs stockpiled over in the next county. So there's a good chance you'll get your walnuts back."

"That's the best news of all," she said with a trace of a smile.

"I'm returning Pickett's truck to his farm," Willie said. "Just thought I should let you know what happened."

Henry saw the opportunity to get away from Sarah for a while. "Maybe I could ride along," he said. "To see Evan," he added, careful not to look in Sarah's direction.

"Sure," Willie said, "if you don't mind walking back."

"I don't mind," Henry said.

They climbed into the truck and went clattering down past Franklin's farm. It was hard to talk above the truck's roar, but Henry was able to point out the spot where he and Evan had slid down into the road the day before. After following the gravel road for more than a mile, they turned into a narrow weed-lined lane. The frame house with its front porch was pale green beneath an ageless layer of dust. Behind the house stood a deteriorating barn and a wagon shed open on both ends.

Just as Willie turned off the motor, Evan appeared at the door. He swung the screen door wide and hobbled out onto the porch on his crutches. Mary Beth came close behind him, along with three smaller children who stared, wide-eyed, from the porch shade.

"The sheriff just left," Evan told Willie. "He said you'd be bringin' the truck back."

"I'm awful sorry about things," Willie said. Evan nodded, his glance shifting to Henry, then away.

Mrs. Pickett's face was a gray, indistinct shadow through the screen. "Won't you come up on the porch?" she said.

Willie walked over to the steps. "I'm awful sorry, Mrs. Pickett."

"You're kind, seein' as how you're the one that's been wronged," she said, stepping out on the porch.

As the two of them talked, Evan worked his way down the steps to Henry. Leaning forward on the crutches, he looked at Henry and shrugged his shoulders. "It was bound to happen," he said.

Henry nodded, wishing he could say something to lift Evan's spirits. The family probably would be better off without Pickett, but he knew he couldn't say that. When they were trapped in the mine, Evan had said he wanted to leave, to get away from his father. He got what he wished for, Henry thought, but not quite the way he'd expected. By the time Pickett got out of prison, Evan would be grown up. He seemed older already.

"Soon as I git off these crutches, I'm gonna look for a job," Evan said. "We got corn planted here and over on the Morrison place, but we'll need money 'fore it's ready to pick."

"Maybe Franklin would hire you," Henry said. Maybe Sarah would, too, when I'm gone, he thought. He started to tell Evan he was going home at the end of the week. "Today Sarah —"

"I gotta take care of the family now," Evan cut in. His eyes burned with determination. Remembering Evan's tireless labor in Franklin's hay field, Henry knew the family would be all right.

"How are your legs today?" Henry asked.

"They don't hurt much anymore," Evan replied, "but Doc said I should use the crutches till Friday. Wayne told me last night his hay'll be ready next week. I'll be back to normal by then. You're gonna help, ain't ya?"

"I can't," Henry said. "I'm going home Saturday."

"Home! What the heck for?"

"Sarah says . . . I'm too much worry."

"Is it 'cause of the mine?"

"I guess so," Henry said.

"Hell, she never did like kids," Evan muttered. "Anyway, I reckon it's my fault you ended up in the mine."

"No, I was the one that decided to climb down there," Henry said.

Evan frowned and looked off down the lane. "Maybe you'll be back this way sometime."

"Maybe," Henry replied. Even as he spoke, Henry felt

the hopeless weight of the truth. He'd never be back. No matter how insecure he felt back there with the Compton family, Gorleyville was still the only place he could claim as home.

Willie came over to the boys. "I guess we'll go, Henry."

"Much obliged for bringin' back the truck," Evan said.

"Sure. If I can help you with anything, let me know," Willie replied.

He strode off and Henry started after him, but then stopped and looked back. He wanted Evan to know that he was sorry about his father, that he hated to leave the valley, that he was glad they were friends. But the words wouldn't come.

"I'll be seeing you," was all he said. Then he turned and trotted after Willie, deliberately not catching up until he had blinked away the tears.

They walked out into the main road without speaking. Willie's shoes crunched the gravel with a steady, soothing rhythm, and Henry found himself trying to match the big man's steps.

"Something on your mind, Henry?" Willie said at last.

Henry's head came up, and he spoke what had been on his mind ever since breakfast. "I'm going home Saturday."

"You're leaving? Is there something wrong at home?"

"Nope . . . something's wrong here. Sarah told me I have to leave. I guess when I went down in that mine shaft, it was too much for her."

Willie thought about Henry's words for several moments. "She was frantic when we were digging, but it's hard to believe she'd send you home just because of that."

Henry could still see the veiled expression in Sarah's eyes when she'd told him he would have to leave. Though she might have regretted sending him away, she'd done it just the same. But even her cold strength could not make Henry hate her. His voice was almost a whisper when he asked Willie the question that had been haunting him.

"Am I her son?"

"What?" Willie asked, but the obvious lack of surprise told Henry he'd already considered the idea.

"Am I?" Henry repeated. He didn't expect Willie to have the answer. All he knew was that the man would understand how important it was for him to learn the truth. But Willie's next words were as jolting as an earthquake.

"To tell the truth, Henry, Sarah asked me the same thing."

Henry stopped still. "She . . . she what?" he stammered.

Willie's arm encircled his shoulders and a gentle pressure urged him forward. "It was the night we were digging in the shaft," Willie said. "She asked me if you were her son. You're probably wondering why she'd ask me. But you see, Henry, I know as much about Sarah's child as she does. When I told you about the young couple getting Sarah's baby, I didn't tell you everything. That couple . . . it was my daughter and her husband."

It took a moment for Willie's words to register, then Henry's mind went racing on. "So he's living with them?"

"No, Henry. There was an accident."

"Accident!" he echoed. Spirits sinking with every word, Henry listened as Willie related the tragic tale. Willie's daughter and her husband had waited at a crossing for a train to pass, then, thinking it safe to cross, had driven their car into the path of an oncoming train traveling a second, parallel track. Both were killed. The terrible loss was there in Willie's face even now. And all the time Henry had thought of him as carefree and lighthearted, a smiling, easy man who helped others in need because he had no problems of his own.

"Then the baby —"

"The baby wasn't with them. He had stayed with some friends that day."

"But what happened to him then?"

"My daughter's friends told me they would like to keep the baby, and after a lot of thought, I agreed to it. They had two children and they seemed such a happy family. I decided they could provide a better home for him than I could." Willie lifted his hands, palms upward. "As it turned out, they gave him up, too, when the depression got so bad. But I didn't hear about that until several years later."

"Does Sarah know all this?" Henry asked.

"After we became friends, we discussed the baby. When I told her the family had given him up to a children's home, she made up her mind to try to get him back. But there were just too many dead ends. We couldn't find him."

Henry had been waiting and hoping for some evidence

that he was, or was not, Sarah's son. He told himself he could accept it either way, so long as he knew for sure. But Willie's story left his question still unanswered.

"I told Sarah I didn't see how you could be her son," Willie said. "Things like that just don't happen."

"Except in fairy tales," Henry finished with a wry smile. He had to agree with Willie. The circumstances were too improbable, the chances one in a million.

"But I can't understand why she'd want you to leave when you've made such a difference in her life," Willie said.

Henry wondered why Willie could think her life was any different. She hadn't changed. She was still Sarah, cool and quiet and remote.

"She needs someone here with her," Willie continued. "This business about the mine is just foolishness. Would you like to stay, Henry?"

"Yes, but —"

"Have you told her that?"

"It wouldn't make any difference. She doesn't want me here anymore."

"You might be surprised," Willie said.

They walked on in silence as Henry's mind whirled with the astonishing facts he'd just heard. Franklin's barn loomed up on their right, then they were past it, traversing the last stretch of road to the Morrison place. When Henry turned into the lane, Willie went along with him.

At the edge of the porch Dandy lay watching their

approach, his front paws curled under him, the sleepy eyes giving no hint of his secret thoughts. Sarah appeared around the corner of the house, and her thoughts, behind her distant eyes, were no more readable than Dandy's.

"How is Mrs. Pickett?" she asked Willie.

"She's going to be all right. I think she's been expecting this," Willie replied.

Sarah went up the steps and sank onto the porch swing. "I'll go over in a few days," she said. "I'm going to have lots more tomatoes than I'll ever use. Maybe she'll want some."

Henry dropped down beside Dandy, rubbing the kitten's ears and realizing for the first time that he would have to leave Dandy behind. Mrs. Compton didn't allow pets. He took the kitten into his lap, knowing all the while he was simply trying to avoid looking at Sarah. He dreaded seeing in her face the knowledge of the secret they'd been keeping from each other. But, he reminded himself, there was no real secret. Willie had said it couldn't be true. If there was just some way to know for sure. Henry looked up and saw Sarah studying him.

"Wayne came by today to see if you would help him with the hay next week. I told him you were going home." Her tone was matter-of-fact at first, but as she continued, the corners of her mouth drooped and her voice faltered. "I wish you could stay . . . but the accident . . ."

"I didn't mean to cause you trouble," Henry started, but he knew she would not, or could not, understand.

How could she know what it had been like at the top of that shaft, alone, terrified for Evan, helpless. "If you'd been up there, you would've tried to help him, too."

"Not that way. It's a wonder you didn't die!" For the first time since he had met her, Henry saw tears in her eyes. It seemed as though he was always causing her trouble. At least when he left, he wouldn't hurt her anymore. And once he was gone, she could return to the smooth, peaceful life she'd had before.

The two of them had forgotten Willie until his sober voice came between them. "Sarah!" He spoke her name with all the quiet command he would have used on an erring sergeant. "This concern about the mine is just an excuse to avoid the real issue. What's bothering you is that you believe Henry is your son."

There was a wrenching sound from Sarah as if she had been suddenly, terribly frightened. The secret was out in the open at last. Henry could hardly bear the awful silence that followed. He did not look up until he heard Willie draw a long, deep breath.

"When is your birthday, Henry?"

At once Henry understood the implications of the startling question. If he and Sarah's baby had the same birthday, it would be fairly certain proof that Henry was her son. For a long moment he considered which would be better, a lie or the truth.

"April first," he said in a quivering voice.

Willie's gaze turned on Sarah, gentle but compelling. "What day was your baby born?"

It seemed to Henry that it took ages for Sarah to respond, but when she did, her chin rose with confidence and her level gaze was surprisingly clear. "April fourteenth," she said.

Henry expelled the breath he'd been holding. A faint sadness enveloped him, and like the flame in an empty lamp, his hopes flickered and died.

"Well, that settles it then," Willie said. "Is there really any reason to send Henry home?"

Henry dared not look up, but he could feel the tension in the air, and he knew Sarah's rejection was only a breath away. As the silence dragged on, he lifted his head. Sarah's gaze rested on him, and there was confusion in her eyes, and pain. One hand fluttered upward to touch her lips, then dropped into her lap again. Finally her features softened in a trembling smile.

"I never wanted you to go, Henry. It's just when I thought you were my son . . . I knew I could not be forgiven for what I'd done."

Henry stared at her, wanting to say he could forgive her anything, but knowing he could not trust his voice.

"Right from the start, Henry . . . that first night when you carried your plate over to the sink, I think I realized that you would change things for me. And you have."

She stopped, but her eyes never left Henry's face. "I don't want you to leave . . . now or when summer's over, either." Henry could hardly take in those words before she was off again.

"I'm not just looking for someone to work the farm,

and I'm not looking for someone to replace my son. You and I, Henry, we've had to make our lives wherever we were sent. Now I think we could make a good life here. Together."

She was right, Henry thought. Someone else had always decided where he would live. For the first time in his life he could make that choice for himself. In that moment, his mind snatched again at the wild hope of being her son; maybe the home had gotten his birth date wrong. Then he brushed the thought aside. Being friends was enough.

He gazed at Sarah and Willie, these two people who had come to mean so much to him, and knew he would stay. There would be no objections from any of the Comptons except Walt and Jack. And maybe Sarah would let them come to visit.

Sarah must have read the decision in his eyes because she came and sat down beside him. Then her arms closed around him. Dandy was squeezed in the dark warmth between them and seemed to enjoy the closeness because he made no attempt to free himself. As his contented purring filled the quiet, Henry looked across at Willie and smiled.